D1553084

RIGHT AND A WRONG WAY TO LOVE A DOPEBOY

LATOYA NICOLE

DEDICATION

I NEVER THOUGHT I WOULD HAVE TO SEE WHAT LIFE WOULD BE LIKE WITHOUT YOU. THIRTY YEARS NOWHERE SEEMS LIKE ENOUGH TIME. YOU SAVED MY LIFE AND TOOK ME IN, WHEN THE WORLD HAD BECOME DARK AND COLD. MY HEART HURTS AND I DON'T KNOW WHAT TO DO TO EASE THE PAIN. YOU WERE THE FIRST PERSON TO SHOW ME WHAT IT REALLY MEANS TO LOVE. WHO IS GOING TO GIVE ME ADVICE AND PRAY FOR ME? WHO IS GOING TO CURSE ME OUT AND TELL ME THEY LOVE ME ALL IN THE SAME BREATH? I DON'T KNOW WHAT TO DO WITH YOU GONE, BUT I WILL CONTINUE TO LOVE YOU. I MISS YOU SO MUCH AND YOU HAVEN'T BEEN GONE LONG. I LOVE YOU GRANNY PANNY DON'T YOU EVER FORGET IT. RIP BESSIE JOAN YATES.

My daughter has been my saving grace without even know it. She has brought me so much joy, and all that matters in this world is her. No one could ever fathom how I feel about her, but I try to explain it every book. So many people have turned their back on her. Treat her like she has the plague, but her uniqueness is what makes her beautiful. You don't have to understand her, just sit back and let her fill your heart with love. My Miracle Monet Riley. An angel walking the earth. My everything. I will forever be grateful, and as long as I have breath in my body, I will give you the world. I love you babes. Mommy loves you.

ACKNOWLEDGMENTS

Every book I try to acknowledge everyone that has been so much to me. Just know as a whole, I am forever grateful to all of you. If I forget to acknowledge your name, know it's not intentional, and there is always next book. Lol I love my support team so much, just know you are the reason that I am me.

To my bookie boos, it's so much said about this group, but you have given so many people so much help and support, I appreciate the hell out of you. The challenges, spotlights, take overs, promo days all of that helps and just know Latoya Nicole appreciate yall.

Law aka Bestie I just want you to know that I'm proud of you and how you are dedicating yourself to school. That's rare now days and I love it. Working and school, both full time is amazing. Keep pushing and you will reach your goal sooner than you think. I'm here for you whenever you need me.

Zee Bae, I don't know another way I can tell you thank you, but I will try. You never tell me no and I will forever be grateful for that. I am probably the hardest person to test read for, but you do it with a smile never getting mad no matter what madness I take you through. I love you and I appreciate you bae. Don't ever forget that. You're an amazing sweet person and I love you for real.

Krissy you just took a spot in my life. Thank you for being there for me no matter what time it is. I love you and thank you for helping me make sure my book is great.

Laci, thank you boo for just always being there. I love you and I just want you to know that I appreciate you. You're always there and I love that. You had my back so much with this book, you have no idea how much I appreciate you. Love you boo.

Kb Cole your ass been missing in action, but I know what it is. I love you and my niece, and I appreciate you being my friend. You are amazing, and I love you Yall check out her catalog.

A.J Davidson your ass helped me so much, I thank you for being there. I don't know where I would have been without you. I appreciate you cousin for having my back. You're a great person and an amazing author. Yall check out her catalog. Welcome baby Andrew aka baby apple I can't wait to meet you.

Annitia chile you are just awesome. I love ya girl and keep pushing. I'm glad you chose me to be your AG.

Anthony M. You know you are my rock. You push and motivate me even when I don't want you too. Thank you for everything that you have been to me all these years. Hopefully Fat Fat made you proud. I'll continue to push myself to be the person you want me to be.

To my family Steph, Malik, Johnnae, Shunta, Shenitha, Sheketta, Sheena, Antronna, Jennifer, Ebony Bae… thank yall for supporting me no matter what. I love yall.

Dawn (Courtney) I love you boo, and I thank you for always supporting me. I appreciate you always.

Victoria, I appreciate everything you do for me and I just want you to know that I notice it. I love you boo.

TO MY HG4L CHAT I TRULY APPRECIATE AND LOVE ALL OF U. WE HAVE BONDED LIKE CRAZY AND YOU'RE STUCK WITH ME FOREVER. SANDRA, SHONTEA, ERICA, MARLA, LIZA, BRIA, KIRSTEN, ATIBA, JARIELLE, ANDRE LASHIA, KAA, MISHA, SOMMER, AND RHIAN

HAPPY BDAY TO MY TWIN BABY JOHNNAE MARKS I LOVE YOU TO PIECES.

HAPPY BDAY TO MY AUNTIE A'SHUNTI I LOVE YOU AND YOU BETTER KNOW IT. BOTH OF YALL GROWN NOW

MY FIRST LOVE

ROUGE YEAR 2006...

"Raven, why do it always take you ten hours to get ready? You broke as hell, so I know you don't have any clothes to go through. Taking all day like you holding some shit in there."

"Shut up. It's not like you going to class anyway. I had to put my make up on, but I'm ready now." Shaking my head, I looked at all the shit she had caked up on her face. Raven was my best friend, but even she knew she wasn't the best looking girl out there. Shorty hadn't grown into her looks yet and got teased a lot, but I still didn't like how she put all that gook on her face.

We've been living next door to each other since I learned how to walk. Our parents couldn't break us away from each other then and they still couldn't now. I had to keep my feelings under wrap, because shorty wasn't checking for me like that. Shit was hard as hell at this age to be around her all the time and not try anything. Even though she wasn't all that cute, her personality drew me in. Her body was banging and now being a teenager that knew his body, it took everything in me to keep my dick down when she was around. Raven was the touchy feely type and loved to lay and jump all over a nigga.

"School ain't for everybody and as slow as you are, your ass should be ditching with me. Let's go on a date or something, fuck school." My ass was laughing, but I was dead ass. It was hard trying to transition from the friend zone.

"You tried it. Your parents don't give a shit what you do. My mama will beat my ass all over that school. Plus, I need you to buy me lunch today." Reaching in my pocket, I gave her five dollars. It was all I had, but I would never tell her that. Like any other day when I gave her my last, I would go out and steal some shit for me to eat. I lived with my parents, but like most families in the hood, our asses were broke. I never allowed Raven to see my struggles, because I wanted her to know I had her. Funny thing was, no matter what I did, she did not see me as anything but a friend. Even though the shit had begun to sink in, it didn't stop me from trying.

"Go inside, I'll be out here when school let out to take you home. Try and pay attention today shorty, one of us gotta make it." Leaning in, she kissed me on the jaw and took off running in her lil ass skirt. Seeing my homeboys waiting for me at the corner, I made my way over there. These niggas were gambling throwing their money away, and I was trying to make some.

"If you done chasing up behind that pussy that you're never going to get, you can get next. I'm after all the money and yours is not an exception." My homie Trippy always gave me shit about Raven. He was the only person that knew I was in love with her. The rest of my niggas thought I just wanted to be the first one to hit.

"I gave shorty my money, so get your Holiday Heart looking ass up. Got me ready to go steal a bike bitch. Let's go, I'm hungry as hell."

10

"You do look like a nigga in a wig. Rouge I walked in on his OG pressing his shit. Nigga was in there jumping like a bitch. Lift his hair up, I bet you see some burns and shit." Laughing at Tim, I walked over and pulled Trippy's hair up.

"Nigga is that butter on your shit?" His ass smacked my hand away and stood up.

"My girl put it on there, said it's supposed to stop the blistering. I beat the shit out of my mama and took her car, so we have a ride today. Let's go get this money."

"It looks like the shit is cooking your naps. What store we hitting up today?" Trippy had this weird ass smile on his face.

"The gas station on Gladys and Cicero. It's so much traffic over there, we can slide right out and jump on the expressway. Easy money and we won't have to do this for a while." Looking over at Tim, I was trying to read his face. That nigga looked like he was about to shit a brick.

"I'm not with that shit bro. Usually we just hit up some lil small ass corner store to survive for a few days. You trying to get

11

us real jail time. Nigga you should be scared of the booty house, you already looking like somebody's midnight lover."

"Yeah, I'm with Rogue on this one. Let's stick to what's been working. You trying to do some new shit and gone get all of us popped. I can't go to jail, I'm the pretty one out of the crew. They gone play double dutch in my ass first." Tim looked to me to back him up, but he was preaching to the choir.

"Aren't you tired of giving your fake girl your last five dollars? As soon as you give it to her, we have to go rob a store just for your ass to get a snack. You too old to be out here stealing snacks my nigga. Don't get me started on Tim. When his ass steals the shit, he has to split it with his crackhead ass mama. Knowing damn well she gone go sell her portion." His ass made sense, but something about the shit just wasn't feeling right. A nigga needed more money, especially since I was trying to take care of Raven as well. Weighing all the pros, I said fuck the cons.

"Aight, I'm in. If this shit goes wrong, imma slip slap your ass. Tim we gone be good bro, if not. We selling Trippy to the highest bidder on the yard. A nigga with a bang gotta go for a lot

in the booty house." Laughing, we jumped in his mama's car and

headed to the unknown.

As soon as the car was parked, I knew shit had gotten real.

He gave us a mask and a real gun this time. Tim looked as if he

was about to bolt on our ass and I tried to give him a reassuring

look. Putting our mask on, we got out of the car and walked into

the gas station. It wasn't any customers and I was glad for that. It

didn't have to get messy.

"Imma need all the money you have in this bitch. If you

want to walk out of here alive, just do as I say. Try to be slick,

imma push your shit back." The Arab behind the counter didn't

look moved and I knew some shit was about to go down. He

opened the register to give up the money and we were watching

him so intently, we never noticed the other guy come out of the

side door with a shot gun. Tim took off running and the guy shot

him. Trippy was shooting back as he ran out of the door, and I

couldn't bring myself to leave Tim. The only reason he was there was because I reassured him that it would be okay. Laying my gun on the ground, I crawled over to Tim trying to see if he was good. The worker kept his gun pointed at me, but he didn't have to, I already knew I was booked.

Tim stopped breathing in my arms and I felt like shit. He was dead because of me and there was no going around that. Raven was going to struggle harder because I was gone, and that killed me the most. I was always her protector against the other kids at school and I fucked up. All for a few extra dollars. We could have planned this shit out and did it the right way. I've always been a thinker and if I put my mind to it, I knew how to figure some shit out.

Hearing the sirens had me fucked up in the head. If I had listened to Raven and gone to school today, my ass wouldn't be on the way to jail. I didn't have bond money and there was no way my mama was gone say fuck the bills to get me out. It was over for my ass and I had to deal with the shit.

14

The police came in and cuffed me. They were reading me my rights, but I couldn't take my eyes off Tim. Out of all the shit we did, I never thought one of us would die behind the stupid shit. The bitch ass police pushed my ass in the car and I knew my life was going to be changed forever. As soon as they pulled off, I heard another officer talking on the radio.

"We got the other suspect. He was pulled over in a stolen vehicle." That was all I heard over my thoughts.

RAVEN...

Walking in the school, I did everything I could to make myself look sexy. I was tired of them talking about how ugly and bummy I was. Rogue did whatever he could to stop them, but them bitches was mean. I tried as much as possible to fix my appearance, but it seemed as if nothing was working. So, the only other thing I could do was come with barely any clothes on. My mama didn't have much money, so it wasn't like me being fly was an option. If I didn't have shit else, I had a body. Why not use that to my advantage? It's not like I was fucking. My ass wasn't nowhere near ready to have sex, especially since Rogue didn't give me the time of day.

I was like a lil sister to him, but every time I was around him, I had to fight the urge to kiss him. The way he licks his sexy full lips always did something to me. He was that deep brown complexion with a low cut and the prettiest smile. I had no idea when I went from looking at him as my brother, to wanting him in the worst way. All I know is one day I woke up and his ass was bae in my mind.

"You looking sexy today Raven. You should come hang out with me for first period." This guy named Keenon interrupted me from my thoughts. He was one of the popular guys in school. Keenon wasn't Rogue, but he was sexy as fuck and all the chicks wanted him. The fact that he wanted to hang out with me had me ready to throw it all it away.

"Hang out where? You know Mr. Keith don't be playing that shit. He knows all the hangout spots and my mama will kill

16

me if I get detention." Walking over to me, he ran his finger down my face.

"Me and Mr. Keith got an understanding since I'm the star of the basketball team. We good. Just come on, I got you." It was only one period, so I figured what the hell. All the bitches were going to hate me for real once they realized Keenon was at me. From the direction we were headed, I could tell he was taking me to the auditorium. When we walked in, I started to get nervous because it was so secluded. Realizing how nervous I was, he grabbed my hand. Sitting down, he pulled me onto his lap.

"I think I'm going to go to class. We shouldn't be here, and I don't want to get in trouble. Maybe we can hang out during lunch." You could see the irritation on his face, but I wasn't feeling this scene.

"I said I got you. How many more chances you think you will ever get like this? Just chill out, I got you." I tried to relax, but my anxiety was killing me. I knew it was really time for me to go, when a group of his friends walked in.

17

"Yeah, I'm going to get up with you later." I tried to get up, but he snatched me back down.

"Naw, my time is money and you not about to waste my shit. You came in here with me, so you must want this dick."

"Dick? I'm a virgin. I just want to leave." His friends surrounded us, and I could feel the tears building up in my eyes.

"Hold her down, she trying to play like she don't want it." His friends grabbed me, and I figured maybe I wasn't making myself clear.

"NO. I DON'T WANT IT AND I WANT TO LEAVE. LET ME GO. PLEASE, JUST LET ME GO." I could feel Keenon trying to relieve his dick from his pants and I started screaming like I was crazy. One of his friends punched me in the mouth and I knew that was a warning.

"Shut the fuck up before I beat your ass." When Keenon pushed me forward, I knew he was about to enter me. Feeling him push inside of me, I screamed out again. It was nothing I could do since it hurt so bad. Grabbing me around my waist, he

18

pumped in and out of me not caring about my tears and pleas. I said no and stop the entire time he was inside of me, but it seemed to only make him want me more. I thought it was only about Keenon, until his friend pulled his dick out and tried to force it in my mouth. I kept turning my head screaming no, but his other friend held my head still.

"Open your mouth and if you bite my shit, imma knock your teeth out." Shoving his self in and out of my mouth, him and Keenon started groaning at the same time. When I felt the liquid in my mouth and coochie, I was relieved. Keenon pushed me off him and fixed his clothes.

"When yall done with her, meet me in the gym. We been there together the entire time, so hurry up. That pussy good and tight, but I warmed it up for you. I wanted to pass out when the remaining guys pulled their dicks out. I screamed the entire time, but none of it mattered. They all took a turn on me until they all came. Leaving me lying there, I cried as I grabbed my phone. Dialing Rogue's number, I called him back to back twenty times.

19

His ass never answered, and this was the first time I think I hated his ass. When I needed him most, he wasn't there. Fixing myself as much as I could, I grabbed my stuff and walked to the main office. I told the clerk what happened, and they called my mother up to the school. Sitting there feeling ashamed, I waited until my mother came and got me.

****

My mother walked in the office mad as hell. I was thinking to myself, she about to turn this school upside down. When she turned to me, I prayed I read her expression wrong. She looked disgusted, but only when she turned my way. The principle waited until she sat down before he began talking.

"Your daughter came to school half naked and enticed the basketball team. They all said that she begged them for it because she was trying to be popular. Now that none of them want her, she is in here crying rape. These are very prominent students, and we will not tolerate these kind of allegations." Standing up, I went off. It felt as if my face was on fire.

"What? Why would I entice half the damn team? They raped me, and it shouldn't matter what I had on. I didn't deserve what they did to me."

"Shut up Raven. Just shut your ass up right now. If you didn't want anyone trying to have sex with you, why the fuck would you walk out of the house looking like a damn hooker?" I couldn't believe she was saying this shit.

"Are you serious right now? Yall are victim shaming and that shit ain't right. It does not matter what I had on, I did not deserve what they did to me." The principle shook his head.

"We are suspending Raven for ten days. If anything like this happens again, we will expel her. We will not tolerate her kind of behavior here. Maybe next time you can monitor your daughter and make sure she is dressed like a sixteen year old and not a whore." The tears fell from my eyes and I just wanted to get out of there.

"It won't happen again sir. Raven, let's go now." Snatching me up, she walked me out of that school as if getting raped was my fault. Those guys will never pay for what they did because all they cared about was that stupid ass basketball record. When we got in the car, I thought my mama would apologize, but she didn't. She hit me with some news I would never have expected.

"I'm sorry Raven, I can't look after you and be at work. I'm not raising a hoe, so you are going to live with your aunt in Atlanta. You're not about to be out here embarrassing me." I didn't say a word, all I could do was cry. When we pulled up to the house, I jumped out and ran over to Rogue's house. He would know what to do. Banging on the door, I screamed his name, but no one came. Feeling my head snatch back, I couldn't believe my mama was trying to fight me.

"Now you trying to fuck him? Bring your ass on. You have twenty minutes to pack or I'll drop your ass at the airport with nothing." Storming in the house, I went to get my stuff. I didn't want to live with anyone who would treat me like this. Fuck her.

GOD'S PLAN

ROGUE YEAR 2018...

Sitting in my Bentley, I pulled on my blunt as a shorty off the block gave me some neck work. It was alright, but my girl's shit was better. Shit like this had me trying to figure out why I still played around in these streets, because these hoes wasn't worth it. It's like it was expected of me to have hoes, so I went with the motions.

A lot has happened since I went to jail back in the day. I served three years for that shit, and when I came home, my mama was about to lose the house. Knowing robbery wasn't my thing, I did what every other nigga in the hood did when shit got rough, started selling drugs. I hustled day and night and gave every dime to my mama. What people saw as one hell of a grind, was really desperation on my part. I couldn't have my mama out here homeless.

23

I slowly moved my way up the ladder and nine years later, I was the right hand to the biggest nigga in the city. Life was good, and a nigga was on top. I even had a bad ass shorty, but no matter how hard I tried, I couldn't be faithful. I always felt like when a nigga found the right one, they wouldn't see another chick. So, it was San's fault why I was this way. If she was everything she was supposed to be, my ass wouldn't be out here getting whack ass head right now. Taking another hit off my blunt, I laughed at my logic.

"You like this daddy? You like the way I suck on this pretty ass dick?" Exhaling, I shook my head no.

"Not really. Try to suck my balls at the same time or something." You could tell she was offended, but I didn't care. If you gone do it, then do it right or get your dumb ass up. When she started sucking like she had an attitude, I pushed her head back. "I'm straight shorty. Maybe I'll swing by later and get some of that pussy, cus this shit ain't it." Smacking her lips, she sat back in the seat. When I looked over and realized she wasn't getting

24

out of the car, I figured she wanted some money. Laughing, I hit

the locks letting her know it was time to make her exit.

"Rogue, you said you was gone get my hair done." She said

that shit in that whiny ass voice I hate.

"Did you finish the job? Then what am I paying you for?"

Before I could respond, I got slapped. Thinking I was tripping, I

thought this hoe turned into an alien octopus because I was hit

from the left. Then I saw San snatching the girl out of my car.

"This the stupid shit I'm talking about. Why the fuck do I

have to be out here fighting bitches over my nigga?" See, I told

this bitch to get the fuck out, now I had to go through this shit.

"Drive nigga before I beat your ass." San had dragged the girl out

of my car and got in. I was getting too old for this shit.

"You do too fucking much. Shorty was buying work and

you just cost me some money. If you don't trust a nigga, then why

you with me?" She had the craziest look on her face realizing she

may have fucked up and just like that, I was in the clear.

"Why the hell you didn't say shit. I was in the car with Liza and I saw a bitch in your car. I wasn't about to ask no questions." Shaking my head, I tried to act as if I was offended by her actions.

"That's the reason why I'm not trying to take this shit further now. I'm in the streets and that means a nigga have to leave any time of the day, take calls, and some nights I might not be able to come home. I can't deal with this kind of stupidity. Where is your car, so I can drop you off? I need to go holla at Lady." San been trying to move in with me for a while now, but I been making all type of excuses. God must have been on a nigga's side because every time she came at me hard about it, she did something and I used that shit to my benefit.

"It's at my house. You know I get the street life shit, but you don't even have to be out there. I'm ready to start a family and you should be too. The streets only gone take you two places." I was so tired of this mufucka trying to put me on the straight path. Her life wasn't even together, but she was always trying to tell me what to do with my shit. I was Fred and that hoe

26

was Grady. I was running my shit and she came over every day riding my train.

"San, if I was ready to have a family I would go in you raw. My kids be on a sliding board going down your throat. They be having fun too. Why would you want to take that from them?" You could tell she was pissed.

"Fuck it. You always want to play and shit when I'm trying to be serious. Hurry up and take me home." I was dead ass serious, but I let her think what she wanted. Pushing my gas petal, I took off fast as hell trying to get her to her destination. She said that shit like I wouldn't rocket ship her ass home. When I was approaching her block, I looked at her and she seemed hopeful.

"Gone head close your eyes and click your heels three times. When you open them, you will be at home." Her slow ass opened the door and tried to get out. I slowed down enough to let her get a good roll out and drove off. This was the dumb shit we went through every time she started talking about a family.

Driving to my mama house, I thought about my life up to this point. I didn't want to bring a child into this street shit, but I had enough to walk away. A nigga just wasn't ready to. Lady had been constantly telling me to leave that shit alone before I went back to jail, but I was smart out here. Pulling up to the house, I got out and went inside. The smell of fried fish hit my nose and I danced all the way to the kitchen. As I did the Nae Nae, Lady looked at me and rolled her eyes.

"Stop flinging your funky ass arms all over my food. You're in a good mood, you must have sold a lot of drugs to our black people today." She was always being sarcastic. The shit blew me at times, but I ignored her ass and looked in the pots. "Wash your fucking hands before I burn your ass."

"Your ass don't do shit but cook and talk shit. You need to get out of the house more. Damn. I Just came over here to talk to you about investing some of my money for me." When she scuffed, I knew I was taking my food to go.

"So, basically, you want me to clean your drug money. You know I'm not getting involved in that shit. Only way I'll do it, is if you're walking away from the streets."

"Lady, that's why I'm trying to set up my future, so I can walk away from this shit."

"I'll think about it. I'm surprised you're here." Now I was confused.

"What you mean?"

"Raven is in town for her mother's funeral. That's why I'm cooking, for the repast." The wave of emotions that hit me was unbelievable. I hadn't seen Raven since I got locked up. When I got settled in on my tier, I called home and Lady told me she moved out of town. Three years and I didn't receive one letter or visit from her. I was pissed, but I still came home looking for her. That was my first stop before I went in the house to wash my ass. Her mama told me she hadn't heard from her and slammed the door in my face. All these years, I've been low key pissed at Raven. We were best friends and she vanished without a trace.

29

No explanation or nothing. Yeah, I was in love with shorty, but she didn't know that. All she knew was, I was a damn good friend to her ass since we were kids. Hell, she didn't even send a message to let me know her mama had died. As mad as I was, I could still feel that soft spot for her creeping up.

"I'll go with you to the funeral." Even though she tried to hide it, I could see her smiling. I don't know why she was happy. It's not like me and shorty was about to be together. I had San, and Raven left me at my lowest point. I waited for her to finish up and it only took her ass another hour. I had no idea who the fuck she was trying to feed, but my nerves were bad as shit and I was ready to go.

Finally making it to the funeral, I tried to keep cool. On the outside, I looked just like another person there to pay their respects. On the inside, my heart was beating out of my chest. Scanning the room, I looked all over for her, but she wasn't there. This mufucka didn't come to her mama's funeral. It wasn't like the place was over crowded, but I was kind of high, so I hope I was just over looking her. Standing up, I walked up acting as if I was trying to view the body. Walking over to the family, it was only a few people there. Raven wasn't here, but a woman I didn't know stared at me with tears in her eyes.

Where the fuck did I know her from? She looked familiar as fuck, but I couldn't put my finger on it. Nodding my head, I gave a sympathetic look and sat down. As soon as I sat in my seat, I felt someone's eyes on me. When I looked over, it was the woman. I don't know what it was but looking into her eyes made me feel funny. It's like I wanted to hug her and take all her pain away. Turning away from her, I continued to scan the room for Raven.

RAVEN...

"I'm not going. It's not like she gave a fuck about me anyway. At this point, I'll only be going so people won't ask why I'm not there." My cousin/bestfriend Coi was looking at me like she wasn't buying shit I was selling.

"Friend, I get it. You scared to see Rogue, but you're gonna have to face him at some point. If you don't, you'll never have closure. Trust me, I'll be on standby ready to knock his ass out if you need me to. Now get your ass up and let's go before we're late." Groaning, I stood up and grabbed my purse. The family car was outside waiting. I had been back in Chicago for a week now, but I stayed hidden.

Yeah, I was trying to avoid Rogue, and all I could do was hope he didn't show up to the funeral. I hadn't seen him since that dreadful day. My mama put my ass on a plane and didn't look back. Living with my auntie Cheryl was so much different. She lived in the suburbs of Atlanta and was so much nicer than my mama. Not once did she treat me as if I wasn't hers, and she gave me everything I could ask for. Me and my cousin Coi clicked instantly and that shit was weird for me. I wasn't used to being close to a female, it was always just me and Rogue. They were my lifeline and I wouldn't be here if it wasn't for my aunt and Coi. A month after me moving out there with them, I started to feel sick and got the worse news of my life. Just thinking about it had me

sick to my stomach.

"*Auntie Cheryl, I can't stop throwing up and I passed out*

earlier at school. I need to go to the doctor."

"*Alright, get your cousin I'll take you to the ER.*" We all

headed out and the entire ride, I felt like I wanted to die. The

waiting room was empty, and I was grateful for the small blessing.

They called me in the back and ran all kinds of tests on me. When

the doctor came in, I had no idea what she was about to tell me,

her face looked sympathetic.

"*Congratulations, you're pregnant.*" From the moment

those words left her lips, she knew it wasn't a happy thing. I

couldn't control the scream that left my lips.

"*No, this can't be happening. I can't be pregnant.*" My aunt

and Coi hugged me because I told them my story and they knew

what happened. They were the only ones that believed me and

didn't think it was my fault. Ten minutes later, she was handing

me discharge papers and we were heading back home. It felt as if *my feet weren't even touching the ground. How could I raise a baby not knowing who the father was? A living reminder of the worst day of my life. How could I love a child like that? I'm guessing they knew I needed my space, because the ride home was silent.*

When we got in the house, I went in my room and locked the door. I could hear them knocking trying to check on me, but I just wanted to be alone. I could not stop the tears that fell from my eyes and I wasn't sure that I wanted to. In this moment, I wanted my mother, so I called her.

"What do you want Raven, I'm at work?" Even though she could hear me crying, that didn't matter to her.

"Ma, I'm pregnant. It happened from the day I got raped and I don't know what to do. I can't raise this baby." You could hear the aggravation in her voice.

"You should have thought about that before you chose to sleep with the entire basketball team. What the fuck you thought was gone happen? No sense in calling me, because I'm not gone

raise the motherfucker. I'm at work and if I wanted to deal with

this, you would be here and not there. Go talk to your Aunt Cheryl.

Don't call me unless it's important." When she hung up in my face,

I couldn't believe how she felt this wasn't important. My heart

broke and I was overwhelmed with heartache.

I was raped and violated by a group of my peers and they

got away with the shit. My mama sent me away and didn't want

me. I was now pregnant carrying who knows baby and I can't even

cry on my mother's shoulder. I've been ugly all my life and nobody

ever wanted to hang around me except my best friend, and even

he abandoned me. Each thought hurt me more and I could no

longer take it. Jumping up, I went to the kitchen and grabbed a

knife.

Without hesitation, I sliced straight through my wrists. It

seemed as if the blood wasn't coming fast enough, so I just started

stabbing anywhere I could.

"Ma, oh my God. Raven, what are you doing? MAAAA.

Please Raven, hold on. We're going to get you help. Just hold on." I *could hear Coi trying to talk me through it, but I was slowly fading*

out. Next thing I knew, I was waking up in the hospital.

Feeling the car stop, I knew we had arrived at the funeral. When I got inside, I didn't even go to the casket. It was as if I was numb. This lady gave me away and didn't give a shit about me. Now here I was, looking at her in a casket and I still felt hurt. It still hurt me to lose my mother. Out of nowhere, the goosebumps rose on my arms. I could feel myself sweating and I knew Rogue was in the room before I even saw him. Looking over, there he was. He was looking around and I assumed he was looking for me.

My looks had changed for the better. I was no longer the ugly duckling everyone knew in school, but I still thought he would recognize me. We were best friends for years how did he not recognize me? My emotions got the best of me as he got up and walked to the casket. We locked eyes and my soul shifted, but I was just another face in the crowd to him.

After the funeral, her body was taken to be cremated. I didn't want to deal with the people, but of course I had to be at the repast. Coi held my hand as we walked inside. I had to put on a front as all these people told me how great my mother was. My nerves went haywire again and I knew he was in the room. He was looking around the room and I knew he was trying to find me. Our eyes locked, and I wanted him to remember. I wanted him to feel who I was. When he turned his head, the tears were beginning to fall. Not being able to take it, I took off running. Going into my old room, I laid on the bed and cried.

"You've changed." Jumping up, I looked into his eyes and I had to fight running to him.

"Yeah, I've changed. If you don't mind, I want to be alone right now." His ass did the opposite and walked over to me. His arms wrapped around me and I wanted to fucking melt. "Just go Rogue." Pulling back, he looked at me confused.

"Did I do something to you? Last I checked, you were the one flaw as fuck. I'm confused on how you pissed at me right now." Not wanting to get into it at my mother's repast, I tried to get up and walk out. He grabbed my arm and I just wanted to be

37

out of his presence. His ass was fighting hard to be around now, but when I needed him the most, his ass wasn't there.

"I don't think you wanna do that shit my nigga. Let her go and I won't have to fuck your ass up." Coi was standing there with a pot in her hand and all I could do was laugh. No matter what, she always had my back.

"Girl fuck you gone do with them lil string beans? Maybe you should ask who the fuck I am before you start trying to play captain save a phony hoe." His ass gave me the most disgusted look ever and walked out of the room. Who the fuck was he supposed to be? Last I knew, he was broke as shit stealing out of stores. When I looked down at the pot Coi was holding, I fell the fuck out seeing it was actually green beans in the pot.

"What the fuck was that supposed to do, make him hungry?" She shrugged her shoulders and she laughed as we went back down with the others. Shuttering, I was tripping on how I could still feel his arms wrapped around me.

HEART TO HEART

ROUGE...

It's been a few days since I saw Raven at the repast. Shorty had me feeling some type of way when I saw her. She looked nowhere near like the girl I knew in high school and that shit had me forgetting that I was pissed at her. That was until, she threw me shade. Shorty was acting flaw as fuck, when she was the one that left me doing a bid by myself. I had no idea why she was treating me like that, but I wasn't with it.

When I stormed out, Lady tried to stop me. I left her ass right there. She was straight because her house was right next door. When I went home, San was all over me about why I smelled like another chick and all I could think about was Raven. Her mouth was moving, but I didn't hear a word she was saying. She fought with me all night as I sat there trying to figure out why she was pissed at me. Which is why I was now sitting outside of Lady's house. She had to know something, and I was about to get answers. When I asked her all these years ago to try and talk to Raven, she told me she moved. Her mother had to say something.

Looking at the clock, Lady should be pulling up in a about ten minutes. What I didn't expect to see was Raven walking out of her mother's house, with the smart mouth bitch from the other day. She locked up and put a for sale sign in the yard. Since I was a firm believer in hearing the shit straight from the horse's mouth, I got out and approached her.

"What up Raven, let me holla at you for a second." I don't know if she was scared, or what, but she was shaking.

"She don't have shit to say to you. Come on Raven, we need to get to the airport." Hearing that she was leaving rubbed me wrong. I hadn't seen her in years and I wasn't ready to let her go yet.

"Find you some business before you walk into something you can't get out of. Raven, I said we need to talk." You could tell Raven didn't know what to do, but I was about to make it easier for her. Grabbing her by the arm, I pulled her towards my car.

40

"Let her go or I'm calling the police. She doesn't want to go with you." Shrugging my shoulders, I threw Raven in the car and closed the door.

"Call them, they on my payroll. See how far that gets you big nose hoe." Looking back at the car, I made sure Raven didn't hear me. When I got in, shorty was sitting there with this dumb ass look on her face. "You were going to leave without saying shit to me?"

"I didn't know I was supposed to." Her head was down as she twiddled her fingers.

"Raven, stop acting like a kid and talk to me. What the fuck did I do to you?" Pulling off, I drove towards my house. Her ass sat in my car and didn't say a word. I was gone give her that until we got to my spot. Seeing my phone ring, I looked down and saw that it was San. Fuck. Not about to answer that shit, I laid my phone down. Hearing it beep, I knew she texted.

San: Since you don't want to answer, I'm on my way to your house. We need to talk.

Fuck. Knowing I couldn't have her popping up, I grabbed my phone and called her back. I prayed Raven didn't say anything or get mad. It's not like we were fucking around or anything, but I had enough problems on my plate. It was attitude all in San's voice.

"Oh, now you want to answer. Guess that means you don't want me to come to your shit."

"I'm driving, I'm not even at home. Besides, that's my shit not yours. I don't do the pop up shit. What you want?" Looking over at Raven, I tried to read her demeanor. I could see her shifting in her seat, but she stayed quiet.

"My girl just told me she saw you with a bitch in your car. Why do you insist on making me act up? Do you like when I drag these bitches?" I don't know why women thought that shit was cute.

"I'm not about to go through this with you today. Did you want something else?"

42

"Your ass gone miss me when I'm gone." She hung up and I glanced over at Raven.

"Your girlfriend is needy." Laughing, I nodded my head in agreement.

"That she is. What about you? Do you have a nigga?" When she shook her head no, my dick got hard. Pulling in my garage, I parked next to my other cars and got out. Her slow ass sat there and didn't move. "Get out of the car Raven." Opening her door, I grabbed her and pulled her out.

When she walked inside, you could see she was curious, but not impressed. That told me she was well off and wasn't struggling. San acted an ass when she walked in here for the first time. She took a million selfies in my shit. I let her walk around and give herself the tour and I took a seat. Finally, she came and sat next to me.

"You weren't there for me." It was barely above a whisper, but I heard her. I had no idea what she was talking about. All I have ever done was be there for shorty. I got locked up, what the fuck she wanted me to do, send her my commissary? I decided not to say anything, to see if she would tell me. When I saw the tears, I knew it was something I was missing. I had no idea why Raven was mad at me, but whatever it was, hurt her deep.

"I called you and you was not there for me. I NEEDED YOU. I BEGGED FOR YOU AND YOU WERE NOT THERE FOR ME." I was confused as hell and I didn't know what to say. She was shaking and crying. Moving closer, I wrapped my arms around her hoping to calm her down. "Let me go, I don't need your sympathy. It would have been nice to have it then." Seeing that this was going to get deep, I got up and walked over to my bar.

Pouring two cups of D'usse, I mixed hers with a little cranberry. Sitting on the couch, I passed her the cup and watched her down it. Whatever was going on had her shaken up pretty bad. When I saw her start to calm down, I spoke.

"You obviously feel pretty strongly about what you're saying. Every time you're around me, your ass start crying. I have no idea what you are talking about or why you're mad. We're not

44

kids anymore, and I'm not trying to read your fucking mind. Act like an adult and use your fucking words." Raven got up and started pacing the floor. I thought she was talking to me, but I think shorty was in this mufucka talking to herself. Out of nowhere she stopped and looked me dead in the eyes.

"You let them rape me." What the fuck was she talking about?"

RAVEN...

All of my mother's affairs was in order, but I still couldn't bring myself to leave. It's as if I had unfinished business, but I was scared to handle it. Every time I was around that nigga, it's like my skin caught fire. His ass still did something to me, but I was pissed, and I didn't want to want him in that way.

Even though I resided in Atlanta, I didn't have to rush back for a job. In college, I developed a passion to write and I just started jotting down my thoughts. Deciding one day to write me and Rogue's story, I let a couple of students read it and it blew up

45

from there. Somehow, it got to one of my professors and she got it published. I've been writing since, and it has given me the leeway to do as I please. The shit ain't easy, I'm up most nights fighting through pain, being tired, and trying not to succumb to my own demons. I survived my rape, but you never really get over it. When I step in a club, I'm scared to drink. If I'm walking down a street, I'm scared the person behind me is after me. Even if a guy tries to talk to me, I think he's trying to set me up to rape me.

I'm damaged, but I use it to write my stories. It was easy for me to put it on paper, but not to the person who my heart belonged to. I was nervous and scared as hell to tell Rogue. He was looking at me all sexy like and it caused a war within me. I was trying to get out why he hurt me so bad, but my coochie was conflicted. She was jumping and throbbing every time I looked his way.

His intense eyes had me palpitating and I wanted so badly to kiss him. I had to keep reminding myself that I was pissed at this nigga. I'm sure he thought I was shy and scared to talk, but that was not the case. The only thing I was afraid of, was if I said

something, it would be come get this pussy. I was scared my

mouth would betray me. My ass wasn't quiet because I didn't

know what to say. I was trying not to say what I was really feeling.

"Raven, what are you talking about?" His voice brought

me from my thoughts.

"The day you left. They raped me, and I called you. I called,

and you never came. Whatever you were doing, was too

important for me. When I got home, my mama sent me away and

you still never called. That shit hurt, I thought we were better

than that. I thought we were friends." It looked as if he was

shocked and hurt, but I wasn't feeding into that shit.

"When I left you that day Raven, I went to jail. For three

fucking years. All this time, I been salty at your ass for not fucking

with me. I had no idea what happened to you and you know I

wouldn't have let that shit fly. Come here." I was shaking my head

no, but my legs and feet started moving. He didn't leave me, and I

was mad all this time. The anger went away immediately, and I

47

was now trying to mask my horny. Gliding over to him, I licked my lips, so they could be ready for this kiss I been longing for. Slightly sticking my titties out, I tried to make them look more enticing. When I got to him, I was ready. My eyes were closing, and I leaned in towards him.

"I need you to tell me exactly what happened no matter what it was. Imma need their names too. I have to put faces to these niggas that violated." It's like the record scratched and my horny music stopped. This nigga wasn't trying to give up the dick, his ass wanted all the details. I could see a mufucka flying across the floor diving to pick up my face.

"Okay." Sitting next to him, I gave him the full story of what happened. By the time I was done, my ass was crying and no longer trying to see what his dick felt like. Hell, I didn't want to think about any dick. Out of nowhere, there was a knock at the door. Rogue got up and answered it and I was praying it wasn't his bitch. I wasn't in the mood for no shit, and shorty could get these hands today. I'm already over here looking stupid and shit, after I thought he was about to make a move, I was not trying to be reminded why.

"Yeah mother fucker, you thought I was gone didn't you? Where the fuck is my cousin? Don't make me tear this mother fucker up." It was Coi and all I could do was laugh at her going off.

"How the fuck you know where I live? Calm all that yelling shit down in my house with your big nose ass. I bet you can smell an ant fart in this bitch can't you? Let me find out you sniffed us out." Dropping my head, I got up to put an end to this madness.

"I followed your ass and sooooo I got a big nose. Now what? Don't get mad at me cus my shit bigger than your dick. Them muscles ain't fooling nobody. Whew they are some nice ass muscles though." I laughed as she touched his arm.

"Coi, I'm good. Rogue this is my cousin, let her in." Looking down, I saw she was holding one of those kiddy bats. "Girl what was you gone do with that plastic shit?"

"Sting the fuck out of his ass if he didn't move. They don't break shit, but them bitches sting like a mufucka. This a nice ass house. You got something to eat in here?" Shaking my head, I

mouthed I'm sorry to Rogue. This girl didn't have no home

training.

"Ain't nothing in that bitch, but y'all can order something. I

have some business to tend to, but I want y'all to stay. We have

some catching up to do. Coi, go crazy and order all the food you

need. I know you have to feed that big ass nose of yours."

Reaching in his pocket, he pulled out a stack of money and

handed it to me.

"You lucky I'm hungry and don't wanna be put out or I'll

slap the shit out of your strong back ass with this bat. Whew chile,

that really is a nice strong back." Rogue walked out, and I couldn't

do shit but laugh.

"How you talking shit but lusting at the same damn time?

Make that make sense. Oh, and it was all a misunderstanding. He

never knew what happened and his ass was in jail. So, we good

now." I had to keep up with her to tell her the story, because she

was all over this man's house. Going through drawers and shit.

"At least now y'all can finally hook up. If there is no bad blood, what's the problem?"

"There's a girlfriend." Coi shrugged her shoulders and laughed.

"Well, we just gone have to fix that. It's time for some strategizing and we not leaving until you get your man."

"Girl you got kids? It's okay, maybe it wasn't meant to be."

"They father has them and I can fly back and forth. You need me too. You see how I hooked my nigga, you think I got him fair and square? It's time to go to war hunny. Ol girl ain't gone know what hit her."

IN MY MIND

"Explain to me again, why my warehouse is full of niggas being held, and it has nothing to do with my money?" Slim was bitching, but I wasn't trying to hear it. Yeah, it was his organization, but I ran everything. I don't like the fact that he was questioning me on anything.

"If they're there, it's for a reason. I'm confused on what the problem is." It was a silence as if he was trying to calm himself down.

"Nigga it's a problem, if I say it's one. Who the fuck do you think you're talking to? I asked you a question and I expect an answer."

"And I gave you one. All that tough shit don't move me Slim. I'm not one of these lil flunky niggas that you pump fear in. As long as it's not going to affect you or your business, there is no problem. Everything that goes on in my life don't revolve around your shit. What you saying to me is, if it's not about your shit,

52

then I can't handle it. Now that, I have a problem with. So, what's good?" The phone went silent again, and I stood outside the warehouse waiting for him to respond.

"Your mouth gone get you fucked up. Handle your business and make sure you clean that shit up. If it comes back to me, just know, we have a mother fucking problem."

"Say less." Walking inside, my crew already had them tied up on their knees with their hands behind their backs. Exactly how I wanted them. When I asked Raven for the names, I wasn't just trying to picture their faces. Those niggas think they got away with some shit and now they had to see me. I couldn't help her then, but I was about to give her closure.

The fact that they tried that shit knowing how close we were, was a slap in my face as well. That shit wasn't random, they planned that shit out. Which means, they thought I was some bitch ass nigga that was gone allow that shit. Walking in front of them, I made sure that they saw who I was.

"Hello fellas. Long time no see." It took them a second to realize who I was.

"Rogue, what the fuck man. I haven't seen you in years, what is this all about?" I smirked, and they knew shit wasn't about to go right.

"See, y'all did some shit some years ago and was fortunate enough to get away with the shit because I wasn't there. The thing about Karma is, that bitch always come back. If I had known then, I probably would have just beat your ass. I was only a rough neck." Leaning down to Keenon's face, I made sure he saw me. "The man you looking at today, is a mother fucking monster."

"Please, I was a kid. We were just having fun. I swear we weren't trying to hurt her. Please, just let us go." Laughing, I signaled to one of my boys. The party was just getting started.

"Calm down. I believe you that you were just trying to have fun. It's nothing." I started to walk off and then turned to say one last thing. "They are just going to have a lil fun as well. Gene, when they're done, put a bullet in all of their heads. Start with the old nigga. His ass let them off the hook, so make sure his ass gets it the worst." I had my men pay a gang of trannies to come and rape they ass. They seemed to think it was fun, so let's see how much fun they had getting fucked. When they walked in, I shook my head and felt sorry for their assholes. Them was some big burly looking ass niggas and I laughed as they started screaming. Leaving out, I got in my car and drove off. I wanted to get back to Raven and tell her she can rest a lil easier. It won't change what happened, but at least these fuck niggas didn't get away with what they did to her. She mattered to somebody.

Hearing her tell me what happened, broke me. It took everything in me not to break down. It was hard as hell trying to be there for her and keep my dick on soft at the same time. Shorty was pretty as hell and it didn't help much that I still had feelings for her. Seeing San call my phone, I let out a sigh.

"What up shorty?"

"I'm at home waiting on you. I cooked your favorite meal and I'm lying here waiting to be your dessert. Hurry up." Fuck.

"I'm kind of in the middle of something, can I get a rain check."

"It's okay, I'll pack up and take it to your house. I'll be waiting until you get back." Knowing she couldn't go to my house, I was gone have to go to hers.

"Your ass better do that shit I like, I'm on the way."

"You already know how I get down. Use your key." This was one of the things I loved about San, she knew how to get me right. Shorty did whatever she could to let me know she was down for me. I love her, but we had different views on shit and that made it hard. I wasn't trying to have a kid or move in together right now. Niggas in the streets use your weakness and I wasn't trying to go that route. I fucked other bitches because I could, but my main purpose was to throw niggas off.

Now Raven coming back threw my shit all off. I loved her, but she doesn't want me in that way. Not to mention, I loved San as well. My mind was all fucked up and this was something I had to figure out quick. It had the potential to turn messy and I didn't do mess. When I walked in the house, I could see the food ready on the table. Not really hungry, I ran upstairs to look for San. I would rather have the pussy right now.

When I got up there, I could hear the shower water running. Taking my clothes off, I laid in her bed and got ready for some bomb ass head. When I looked up, I grabbed my gun and shot. It was a shadow of a person and I wasn't taking any chances. Not hearing a body fall, I stood up and walked slowly to the closet door. When I opened it, shorty had a damn wig on a doll head.

"Nigga why are you in here shooting up my hair. That's my good hair. What is wrong with you?"

"I thought somebody was hiding trying some bullshit. Why the fuck you got the damn wig hanging up and shit? Put that bitch in the drawer or something." She laughed and grabbed it off the head.

"Nigga this is Malaysian wavy, she don't go in the drawer. Here, does this make you feel better? I'll put it up here." She hung the shit on the edge of the TV and all I could do was shake my head. At this point, I wasn't even horny no more. Getting up, I threw my clothes on and headed downstairs. Grabbing my food, I put it in the microwave and got ready to eat. Even though it was a wig, this let me know I didn't fully trust San.

Sitting down to eat, I tried to go over it in my head. Would I would have done this if Raven hadn't come back in my life? I think she was clouding my judgment and that wasn't good. Before she came back, me and San were good. We had our problems, but we were still good. I avenged Raven and now it was best I left her where she was. Two women could only end up messy as fuck. It was going to be hard as hell, but I was gone have to stay away from her.

RAVEN...

Me and Coi went over my plan a million times on what to do when Rogue came home. I was supposed to lay it all out on the table, and I mean that in the literal and figurative sense. I took a few shots of liquor and a bunch of pep talks to get me laid up in his bed naked. My ass laid there so long, I fell asleep. When I woke up and saw that Rogue still hadn't come, I got up and put my clothes on. Grabbing my phone, I called Coi.

"Damn bitch, it's been hours. You must have pulled out the swirl and twirl on his ass. You make sure you tell his sexy ass I taught you that shit."

"Girl, ain't shit happen. I'm just waking up and he still not here. All I got is a headache and a stiff leg trying to stay in that sexy position. I'm about to get dressed come get me."

"I'm on the way and don't start that I'm done with this plan bullshit. Phase one is as dead as your leg, but we just gone move on to the next part of the plan." Laughing, all I could do is shake my head. This bitch was crazy, but I was game.

"Alright." Getting dressed, I waited at the door until she pulled up. As soon as I got in the car, she started in with the next part of the plan.

"We need to know when they are going to be at his house together. She needs to see you and know that you exist. Her crazy will start to show and he will get tired of her accusing him of being with you. Next thing you know, his ass gone be crying on your shoulder and boom. You take the dick."

"I don't know how to take the dick. What are you talking about?" She could tell the wording put me in a bad head space.

"I'm sorry Raven, not like that though. Us freaks just use that term. I mean, just start kissing him and shit. Pull his dick out and start sucking it. You know, take it. Don't leave room for him to think about it."

"We'll try one more time, but that's it. I'm not about to be out here steady looking like a fool and his ass not paying me no attention. You didn't see how I leaned in for that kiss and he let my face smack the floor. His ass wasn't on that shit at all." When she laughed, I couldn't do shit but fall out with her.

"That's because you didn't do it right with your slow ass. I still can't believe you tried to get a kiss in the middle of a heart to heart. Girl, you didn't fully explain how sexy that mufucka is. It took everything in me to keep my hands off him. Is my nose really

RIGHT AND A WRONG WAY TO LOVE A DOPEBOY

big though? That nigga ain't got no manners." Laughing, I nodded

my head.

"Bitch who nose." When I said that and shrugged, she had

the shittiest look on her face. My cousin was pretty as hell, but

her shit did look like a passageway.

"Fuck you mmk. Where am I dropping you off to?"

"I'm going to stay at my mama's house until all of this is

figured out. It worked for Monica when she lived next door to

Quincy, maybe the shit will work for me too.

"Bitch bye. Quincy almost got married on that hoe and she

lost the basketball game, I thought it was over for her. She came

close as hell to losing her man. We not gone let it get that far. As

long as you got me helping you, ain't no way you won't get his

ass. I just have one condition. When you get him, you gotta let me

rub his chest for a few minutes." Coi was crazy and I was glad she

was pulling up to the house. If I had to deal with her another

minute, I might have pissed on myself and that shit wasn't cute at

all.

"Bye girl. I'll call you later after I get myself together. I'm gone need to go to the mall to get some more clothes and shit." Hugging her, I got out and grabbed my bag from the trunk. Taking it back in the house, I got ready to shower when my phone rang.

"Hey shorty, I had to run in the gas station to call you. My girl is dead set on coming to my house because she thinks I have a chick there. Are you still there?" This nigga didn't even say hey or try to see how I was feeling. It made me think about what Coi said to me. The next part of the plan was his girl seeing me.

"Yeah, I'm still here. I just got up, I'll be out by the time you get here."

"Thanks shorty. I'll hook up with you later." When he hung up, I called Coi back fast as shit.

"Turn around and come get me. This nigga on the way to the house with his bitch. I told him I was still there, so I need you to get me there before he gets back."

"Bitch, now this is my type of shit. Be at the curb, imma slow down enough for you to jump in."

62

"Girl you got me fucked up." Grabbing my keys, I walked out and went to wait by the curb. Coi pulled up and I waited for the crazy hoe to stop before I got in. The way she took off, let me know I needed to strap up. I held on for dear life and pushed that imaginary break on my side. This bitch was trying to kill me. We were back at his house in no time, but I couldn't tell if he was back or not, since he parked in the garage last time.

"Bitch how am I supposed to know if he's already in there?"

"I'll park down the street and wait for twenty minutes. Go lay in front of the garage and play dead. If he's not already in there, when he pulls up, he will see you."

"Play dead? Bitch what kind of plan is that? What if he's already in there?"

"Girl, you wasting time. I said I'll wait down the street for you damn. Now get out and go play dead bitch but try to look sexy and not a mess." Shaking my head, I got out of the car and shook my head at myself. This was a retarded ass plan and I was not about to lay down there for twenty minutes. Feeling like a fool, I got down on the ground and tried to lay in a sexy position. The shit hurt, and I was over it, so I just laid flat on my back. After twenty seconds, I fell the fuck out laughing. About to get up, I heard a car coming. Lying as still as I could, I pretended like I was dead. The car slammed on breaks and I felt my goose bumps rise. It was definitely Rogue.

"Who the fuck is this bitch?"

"Not right now. Take my car and go to your house. Someone could still be inside. I'll stop by to make sure you're good in a few."

"You think I'm about to leave you with this bitch, you got me fucked up. Who the fuck is she? Why was she in your house Rogue?"

"SAN!!! Go the fuck home. We'll talk about it when I get there." I could hear the tires screeching, so I knew she left. I didn't know if Rogue was still standing there, because he didn't say shit. My ass didn't know what to do at this point. A few minutes later, I felt him pick me up and carry me inside his house. I could feel his

heart racing and I knew he was scared.

"Come on Raven, don't do this to me now. I just got you

back." He laid me on the couch, and I knew it was time to stop

playing this game.

"Whew, my damn back hurt laying on that ground like

that." When I sat up, I saw him standing in the kitchen looking at

me like I was crazy.

"Raven, were you faking?" I couldn't control my laugh

when I saw how shocked he was.

"Hey, I needed to talk to you and your ass was trying to

play house and shit." His ass stood there in disbelief, but I couldn't

stop laughing. In the middle of me falling the fuck out, my head

snapped back. This nigga threw some hard ass buns at me and I

couldn't even get mad. I deserved that shit, but I got my nigga

here.

SORRY NOT SORRY

SAN...

Driving to the house, I was pissed. I knew it was a reason Rogue didn't want me at his shit. If he thought this shit was going down like that, he had me fucked up. I will drag the shit out of that bitch every day. I've put in too much work with Rogue to allow another bitch to take it. Here I was waiting for this mufucka to give me a ring, instead, his ass playing house with some bitch. He barely allowed me to spend the night, how this hoe get in there?

I been rolling with this nigga since he got out. I've stood by him when he didn't have nothing, I'll be damned if she gets him once he's on top. My ass done took all kinds of shit off this man, but I wasn't about to come second to a bitch. From the first time I met him, Rogue has been giving me hell.

"Jen, let's go to the court. It's hot out here so, I'm sure all the niggas out there." We both had our booty shorts on, trying to

pull one of the ballers. That was the thing to do in Chicago. Go to the spots all the niggas frequent in some lil ass tight ass clothes. We weren't any different and I was ready to pull a nigga.

"Bitch come on. My pussy sweating and I ain't wear these lil ass shorts for shit." Laughing, we headed to the basketball court. It wasn't that I was broke, but I wasn't trying to work if I didn't have to. My parents owned a bar and grill, the shit did well, and they have always given me what I wanted. Growing up in that kind of house, I always said I wanted a guy like my dad. Who didn't mind letting his wife sit at home and take care of him, while he brought in the money. I wasn't on no using type of shit, but my daddy set the tone for any nigga in my life.

When we got on the court, all I saw was potential. It was niggas everywhere and I didn't know who to choose. I decided to allow them to come to me. Standing right by the hoop, I posed drinking some water as I had a meaningless conversation with Jen. The ball flew our way, but I wasn't thinking to throw it back.

"Damn, if your loose booty ass gone stand there trying to get a nigga, the least you could do is make yourself useful. Throw the fucking ball or get off the court." Everyone was laughing, and I wasn't one for the slick talk.

"Do it look like I'm the ball handler? Get the shit yourself."

"It looks like you handle all the balls in your jaws. Get your hoe ass off the court." I was so pissed, but Rogue had just gotten out of jail and I wasn't trying to be the reason he went back.

"Fuck you and your balls." Laughing, he walked past me and grabbed the ball. Out of nowhere, he threw the shit at me and I was just gone have to get my ass whooped today. He had me fucked up. Running over to him, I went to slap his ass, but he caught my hand. Grabbing me, he picked me up around his waist and I think I came in my panties.

"You just need some act right don't you? Keep talking shit, imma slide this dick up in you." Before I could respond, his friend yelled out to him.

"Nigga put her ass down. You been in jail too long and shit. I said let's play ball, not play with your balls. Lame ass nigga, let's go." Rogue started laughing and slid me down his body. When I felt his dick caress me from my stomach to my thigh, I was ready to give him some right there.

"Don't go nowhere. We gone finish this conversation."

My ass waited, and I been rolling with him ever sense. I was pissed when I found out he didn't have money like that. He was just breaking into the drug game, so he was a worker. It's been plenty of times, I had to buy our food or pay for us to go out. His dick had me gone and I no longer cared about his money. Once his ass started getting paid, I just knew shit was gone get better. Instead, it got worse. Rogue started feeling his self and other bitches became a problem. He always had some grand ass excuse, but my gut told me I was right.

If I ended up Mrs. Wright, it would all be worth it. He's never chosen another bitch over me; this time was different. It was time for my ass to start strategizing. As soon as I got to the house, my phone rang, and it was my girl Jen.

"Bitch, where the fuck you going? You done stole that nigga's car? I just saw your ass tearing off like a bat out of hell in his shit." Shaking my head, I swear that bitch didn't miss shit. Her ass was always in the loop.

"He gave me the car, because he had some bitch at his shit. Girl, I think I'm gone have to kill this nigga." You could tell she was soaking the shit in.

"Girl what. Who was she?"

"I don't know, she was laying outside his door and he thought somebody was still in his house, so he made me leave. I knew I wasn't fucking crazy."

"Well friend, that don't mean he was fucking with her. Bitch could be his neighbor. You stay jumping to conclusions and he a good nigga. Me and Yo been engaged for two years, and this nigga stay getting caught with a bitch. They know he ain't going nowhere though. I get the money, the house, the cars all that shit.

All these hoes is getting is a wet ass. Don't let these lil hoes win. They know who his bitch is." Jen nigga did her way worse than Rogue has ever done me. She done caught his ass in their house with bitches.

"You're right, but I will never be okay with another bitch fucking him. I'm gone beat they ass every time."

"So, what you gone do? You need to be forcing him to let you move in and you won't have that problem. I keep telling your ass, quit letting him control your relationship. Your ass better get pregnant or something." This bitch always tried to make the shit seem simple. I've been trying the shit. His ass shake out that jam every time I bring it up.

"You know he uses condoms. Oh shit, here he come, imma call you back." I could hear the key going in the door, so I sat on the couch making sure I look pissed. He walked in the door like nothing happened.

"Where my keys at San?" I couldn't believe this nigga.

"That's all you gotta say to me? After you humiliated me and treated me for some bitch, you gone walk your sleuth footed ass in here and act like ain't shit happen. You must think I'm a special kind of dummy." His ass started laughing and I wanted to fight him, but Rogue had that jail body. His ass might knock my wig loose.

"I told you, this is the reason we still live in separate houses. I can't deal with this shit. Where my keys, so I can get up out of here." This nigga thought that shit was gone work, not this time.

"Rogue, I've allowed you to embarrass me out here in these streets. Do what you want and even convince me why we shouldn't live together, but if you don't tell me who that bitch is, we got a mother fucking problem."

"Calm down San, your wig shaking. You all upset over nothing. That's Raven. She was here for her mama funeral. I don't know why she was outside my house." I don't know why, but I got this feeling that shit was about to get all fucked up. He's talked

72

about Raven a lot, and I could see how hurt he was about her ghosting him when he got locked up. If this was some random bitch, I could handle that. Now, I had to compete with a hoe that had his heart all his life.

"When she going back home?" This hoe needed to get up out of our space.

"I don't know. Look, you know that's my best friend. We done talked about the shit from back in the day and it was a misunderstanding. So, I don't want to hear no bullshit if I'm hanging out with her. I don't know when she going back home."

"Oh, we gone hang out while she here huh?" His ass laughed, and I knew what his answer was going to be.

"Naw San. You don't have shit to worry about. Can I get some head now? You doing all that talking, can we do something else with your mouth?" Usually, I would have talked shit, but desperate times, calls for desperate measures. I sucked his dick like I was trying to suck his life through his hole. His ass was so gone, I decided to go for the gusto and see if I could get away with some shit. Getting up, I slid down on his dick and all he did was take in a breath. Usually, he talked shit if I even looked at his dick without a condom. Knowing this was my one and only chance, I couldn't allow him to realize what was going on. Tightening my muscles as much as I could, I rode that dick and pulled that nut out quick as hell. Leaning down to kiss him, I felt hopeful. Maybe this was the breakthrough that we needed.

ROGUE...

Pulling up on the block, I grabbed a blunt and started rolling it. A nigga was stressed, and I was trying to figure out how I got here. My life had been good, and I had no problems. I kept San at a distance and my money flow was beyond enough. I could walk away if I wanted to, but the money was too good. In one week, Raven had come and turned my shit upside down.

Something was different with us, but it could be me just wanting her bad as hell. I haven't tried to get the pussy, because she wasn't into me like that. Besides, I didn't need the

74

complications. San was on my heels hard, since she found out

Raven was here. It was like she always wanted to be around.

Since, she was my girl, I had to show her that her spot was secure.

That was the part that was stressing me out the most though.

Taking a pull, I saw Raven walking around looking like she was

lost.

"Shorty who you looking for?" Turning to my voice, she

smiled and walked over to me.

"I'm not out here looking for a sawbuck. Open this raggedy

ass door and let me in." Laughing, I could tell she hadn't been in

the hood in a while, because she was calling a dime bag a

sawbuck. Hitting the lock, I let her in. "Damn, this car is lit up.

What you in here smoking kush?" Laughing again, I shook my

head.

"When is the last time you been in the hood? You sound

like a B list movie from the fucking nineties."

"Shut up. I don't know how much longer I'm going to be

here, so I figured we could hang out. I don't care about your lil

75

hood rat, today is my day, so clear your schedule." I knew this was

not what I needed, but she was looking sexy as hell. How was I

supposed to tell her no? She was leaving soon, so what harm

would it do for a nigga to hang out with her for a few days?

"On one condition, you gotta hit this. I'm not about to be

riding around high, and your ass acting all high and mighty. Here."

Passing the blunt to her, I didn't expect her to actually take it. She

probably ain't smoked since school. When she pulled on it, it felt

like old times. Shorty started choking and nothing has changed. "I

see you still got virgin lungs. I thought some nigga would have

opened them up by now."

"Fuck you. I can swallow some dick, don't get it twisted.

Since you got me smoking, you definitely gone have to feed me."

My dick bricked up and it was gone be harder than I thought.

"Let me see." Her eyes bulged out of her head and she

choked hard as hell again. Of course I was playing, but when she

started leaning towards me, I almost lost it. When she got close,

she leaned close to my ear.

"Nigga you not ready for this. Stick with your lil girlfriend that probably peck on your balls. I'm a magician, I'll make that shit disappear on your ass. Fuck around and be walking around dickless, stay in your lane Rogue." It took everything in me not to whip my shit out and see if she was really bout that life. Since I knew she didn't like me in that way, I kept my shit in my pants.

"Yeah aight, where you trying to go?"

"I don't know. I haven't been here in years. Give me the Rogue treatment like you do these lil bitches."

"Trust me, you don't want that. Sit your ass back and hit this blunt again. We about to get fucked up for old time sake." When she gave me a smile, I felt funny and shit and I didn't like that. I was high, so I had to really think about some shit we could do. Me and San went out to eat, but we didn't go out too often. I damn sure didn't take these other bitches nowhere. Heading to Hillside Bowl, I decided to take her somewhere I've always wanted to go. A nigga was grown as shit, but I've never been to a damn bowling alley. I was about my money and that shit didn't stop. I could tell she was about to get in her goofy mode. I knew her better than she knew herself.

"Nigga why your ears so big? You always had some big ass mufucking ears. I bet my finger can fit in them." I knew it, goofy shit. Her ass started sucking her finger and trying to put them in my shit.

"Raven gone man. You always do this dumb shit. Imma give your ass some shit to spit on, with your nasty ass." Getting out of the car, I opened her door and she jumped on my back.

"Come on big daddy. You know when I'm high a bitch can't walk. So, carry me inside."

"You so damn spoiled. How the fuck weed makes your legs give out? I was too young to realize it was bullshit back then, but I know your scheming ass getting over now. I should drop you on that fat ass." You could feel her laughing and her titties was bouncing against my back.

"This mufucka is fat ain't it? You wanna touch it?" It was no stopping my dick from breaking my jeans and I was about to let

78

her feel this mufucka. Grabbing her by her legs, I flipped her around and even though was still around my waist, we were now face to face. Putting my hands on her ass, I gripped her shit.

"Yeah, this mufucka is fat." Sliding her down a little, I allowed her to feel that dick. I wanted to see how she would respond, but she said nothing. It was as if she couldn't feel this shit poking out her back.

"Come on and take me inside. I'm hungry and I feel like kicking your ass." Walking her inside, I paid for our lane and went and grabbed some food. While we waited, I grabbed us a couple of drinks and went over to where she was sitting. Shorty was lacing up these ugly ass shoes and handed me a pair.

"Why you putting your feet in them ugly mufuckas? The whole city done had them shits on. I'm not putting them on." Grabbing her drink, she took a sip as she laughed.

"You got it player. All I know is, this is about to be some funny ass shit. What are those, Red bottoms? Yeah, this gone be funny as shit." Ignoring her, I went to get the food. When I came

79

back, she had already set our names up on the board. She had me

typed in as bestie. I don't know why, but that shit pissed me off.

Sitting down, I grabbed a wing and thought about what I was

doing. A nigga was in here torturing myself for no reason.

"You not gone eat your food?" Her ass was just sitting

there drinking watching me and shit.

"These nachos look cool, but I want some of yours. Can I

have a bite?" Grabbing a drumstick, I leaned in to give her a bite.

She wasn't getting one of my flats. Her lips looked sexy as fuck

wrapping around it, I could picture her shit around my dick.

"Man come on and bowl." Shorty was making this hard for

me and I wasn't with the blue ball game.

"You first playa." She was laughing, but I had no idea what

was funny. Grabbing a ball, I walked up to the line and threw it.

What I didn't expect was for me to go sliding down the lane with

it. I'm guessing that was the reason Raven kept laughing. She was

damn near on the floor now. Crawling out of the lane, I saw

everyone laughing and I didn't like that shit. Getting up off the floor, I walked over to the niggas in the next lane and shut they ass up fast.

"If you think that's funny, wait until I shoot the entire bowling alley up." The smile left fast as hell. I went over to Raven and she was wiping tears out of her eyes. "Go get me some of them funky ass shoes. You could have told me with your funky ass. Size twelve." When she got up to go get my shoes, I sat my ass down and rubbed my knee. That shit hurt like a mufucka and low key I was ready to go, but I promised her all day. It did feel good to be hanging out with no pressure. Shit didn't feel forced, with Raven, everything just felt right.

AS WE LAY

RAVEN...

I was higher than giraffe's pussy, but I was having a great time. Everything about today was perfect. Rogue didn't even answer his phone and I was loving the attention he was giving. It was just like back in the day, but we both were grown. It was so easy to fall back into how we were, because we knew each other inside and out. The only thing I didn't remember, was his dick being that damn big. Granted, I've never felt it out right, but I've laid on his lap and stuff.

It took everything in me to act as if that shit didn't faze me. I was praying my pussy juices didn't show through my pants. We had been some of everywhere and now the night was coming to an end. We did Navy Pier and rode the Ferris wheel, ate cotton candy, and even went to a batting cage. My ass stalled him as much as I could, and now he was ready to drop me off. His ass went in the gas station and I made a quick call to Coi.

"Hey bitch, he dropping me off at home. What am I supposed to do? Help me NIGGA." You could hear her laughing, but I ain't have time for that shit.

"Look, tell him you can't find your keys and he have to take you to his house. Better yet, tell him your dead mama freaks you out and you just want a peaceful night of sleep." The latter seemed more reasonable.

"He's coming." Hanging up the phone, I turned on my fake nervous demeanor.

"Aight shorty, we can get out of here now. I hope you had a nice time today. It felt good to just live, instead of business all the time."

"Can I ask you for one more favor? I haven't slept good since I've been in my mama's house. I really just want one well rested night. Can I stay at your place? I'll cook you breakfast in the morning." You could tell he was thinking it over and hard as hell too. If he told me no, I was just going to tuck my tail and go the hell home. There was no way I was going to let him keep breaking my face. I did have a little pride left. Looking at him with pleading

eyes, I waited for his response.

"Aight Shorty." For some reason, he didn't look very happy

about saying yes. I almost told him fuck it and take me home. I've

never felt so defeated in my life. The mood in the car turned blah

as hell and I no longer knew what to say. When we pulled up to

his house, his ass looked so irritated, I barely wanted to go in.

Heading inside the house through the garage, he threw his keys

on the counter and removed his shirt. "I'm about to take a

shower, make yourself at home." He disappeared upstairs, and I

grabbed my phone and called Coi back.

"Bitch I'm here, but he do not want my ass to be. I feel like

a clingy hoe that don't know when she outstayed her welcome.

I'm about to call an Uber and take my ass home."

"Where is he now?" I had no idea what that had to do with

the price of tea in China.

"He went to take a shower. I'm going to be gone by the

time he gets out. Fuck this plan, I feel stupid."

"No bitch, you sound stupid. You done put too much work in and your ass going through with it. Now stand your slow ass up and remove your clothes. Go get in the shower with that man and take control. You too grown to be playing hide go seek with the dick. Show him what he is missing and get what your ass been craving. I didn't stay here for shit. I'm in here riding a vibrator while my husband at home. You better go get some dick for us."

"Okay Coi, but if he turns me down, I promise you, I'm coming to beat your ass."

"If you do it right, he won't turn you down. Don't forget to do the swirl and twirl." I was trying to take everything in, but she was throwing a lot of information at me.

"What the hell is that?"

"Girl, you don't know shit. No wonder your ass is single. A swirl and twirl is when you riding him face first, then you turn around while you still on the dick and start riding him reverse cowgirl. Make sure you do it right and don't bend his dick. Oh, and send me a pic of it. Shit better not be little." Shaking my head, I started removing my clothes. I didn't want him to get out the shower or that will fuck up my plan.

"Bye hoe, I'll let you know how it went tomorrow. Wish me luck." Hanging up, I hurried up and took my shit off. Walking upstairs, I went in his room and heard the shower going.

Well bitch. It's now or never. Go in there and make him want you. Don't worry about your scars, just go.

After five minutes, I finally convinced myself to walk in there. His head was under the water, so I don't think he heard me come in. Stepping in behind him slowly, I didn't touch him until I was all the way in. When I placed my hand on his chest, he opened his eyes and snatched my hands. He was holding them away from his body and I felt like shit. Our eyes locked and the stare alone almost made me cum. Lifting my arms above my head, he pinned them against the wall and came in for a kiss.

I had longed to feel his sexy thick lips against mine for as long as I could remember. His tongue forced its way into my mouth and it tasted so good. I couldn't control my moans. Pulling away, he looked at me again and started washing my body. As soon as the loofah got to my pussy, his mouth was covering mine again. My body started shaking and I wanted him inside me right then. It's like his ass was caressing my clit but cleaning me at the same time. When he stopped to let the water rinse me off, the tension in the room was thick as hell. His mouth went to my nipples and I reached down to feel his dick to see if my mind was playing tricks on me.

It wasn't, that shit was big as hell. I didn't know if I could handle all of that, but I was damn sure going to try. Rogue was sucking so sensual all I could do was sit there with my mouth open. His mouth felt so good on me, I had no idea what took me so long to make this happen.

"You sure you want this?" His voice was low and raspy, and I wanted him in the worse way.

"Yes nigga. You think I'm in here slipping and sliding trying to hold on in this soapy ass water just to stare at your ass? Fuck me shit." His ass smirked and scooped me up. I prayed he didn't drop me as he carried me to the room. Lying me down, he pinned my arms over my head again. Using his knee, he separated my legs and I was ready for what was about to happen. I could feel his tip at my entrance and I braced myself for that big mufucka to go inside. Instead, he slid in slowly and took his time. This was that, I'll get down on my knee and propose to his ass type of sex.

Grabbing my hand, we interlocked fingers and he stroked me slow and strong. Tears fell from my eyes. I never knew sex could feel so damn good. It's like my entire soul was on fire. God had to come down himself and bless this dick. His bitch was gone have to fight me, because there was no way I was leaving this nigga alone. He belonged to me and I intended to claim what was mine.

ROGUE...

It's been a month and Raven was still here. I had no idea what we were doing, but I was a mess. It was as if I had two girlfriends and the shit had me all fucked up. I felt like shit, because I really loved the both of them. With San, it was about time and her holding me down. She was there for me when I didn't have shit. It was almost as if I owed her my love. I've been stringing her all this time and it's like it was only right she got my heart.

Then on the other hand, it was Raven. I've loved her since as long as I could remember. I never thought I would actually have a chance with her and now, shit was different. Everything about us just clicked and the shit felt right as fuck, but I had no idea where her head was. We didn't talk about what happened the next morning after we had sex.

Hell we haven't really talked about it since. We've hung out, but I didn't know how to approach the situation. Since I had a lot of shit on my plate, I didn't want to be the one to bring it up. It would only make me have to man up and choose. I wasn't sure if I was ready to do that yet. My phone rung and brought me out of my thoughts. It was Raven and I found myself smiling looking at her name and pic pop up on my phone.

"What up Shorty? What you got going on today?"

"Nothing, I was on my way to the store and I was trying to see what you wanted for dinner tonight. Do you have a taste for anything special?"

"Surprise me."

"Okay, see you later." That was her way of letting me know she was gone be at my crib. That was another thing I had fucked up with. She was going to the store one day and coming back, so I gave her a key. So far, the shit hasn't caught up with me yet. That can get ugly if Raven uses it at the wrong time. I noticed shorty don't even ask me to come over, when she hit me up, I knew to keep San away.

"Fuck wrong with you nigga. You out here zoned out like you done been hitting that white girl. Get your dumb ass in here, you know Slim don't like to be kept waiting." The lil homie Geno was at my window yelling like I couldn't hear him. Nodding my head, I finished my blunt and headed inside. This nigga Slim was really starting to rub me wrong, but when you the big man, you can do shit like that. I made easy money, and everything was breezy, but the way he came at a nigga sometimes, had me ready to teach that nigga a lesson. His ass was sitting in his chair like he was untouchable. Looking down on the rest of us like we were some peons. Nigga was dramatic as hell if you asked me.

"Nice of you to join us Rogue." I ignored him, and he continued on with the meeting. "We have a new shipment and I want to make sure everybody is doing their part. This is some new shit and it's damn near pure. We not taking no more shorts and the product has gone up. Anybody got a problem with our prices, then they have a problem with us." This nigga was always doing the most and this was just another example.

"Who gone tell them the product has gone up? We got deliveries today and they are expecting to pay what they used to giving us." Geno asked a valid question, but I already knew how Slim was coming.

"You think I give a fuck about what they used to paying? When you take it to the delivery, tell them how much they owe and if they don't have it, then they don't get the product. Simple. The work speaks for itself."

"Aight. I was just saying..."

"You ain't saying shit. Your ass not even on the board of mufucking thoughts. You don't get paid to think, you get paid to drop off packages." Laughing under my breath, I shook my head. I'm glad I wasn't a lil nigga no more. When I was, he wasn't that big in the streets. Now his ass was feeling his self. Since I was his right hand man, it wasn't much he could say to me.

Sensing we were done, I grabbed my normal totes and headed out. I didn't even speak to Slim. I did my normal drop offs and headed over to Lady's house. She had been calling me and if I didn't go soon, she would beat my ass. Using my key, I walked inside, and she was sitting on the couch drinking some wine. When I gave her a kiss, she rolled her eyes at me like I was getting on her nerves.

"If you had an attitude, why the fuck you blowing my phone up Lady? I got shit I could be out there doing, but I stopped what I was doing to see what was up." When she gave me that I

know you not talking to me like that look, I sat my ass down.

"Because I mother fucking can. Don't walk up in my house

questioning me. I heard you and Raven been hanging out and shit,

let me tell you something son. If you haven't closed one door,

don't you open the next one. Now I don't particularly care for San,

but that's who you chose to be with. I don't condone that shit." I

should have known she was on some lecture shit.

"Ma, I'm grown. I think by now, I know where to stick my

meat. Your son grown, I got this. Can I take you shopping or

something Lady?"

"Your big lip ass can't buy me David. I don't want your

dirty ass drug money and your little dirty dick ass better figure out

what you want to do. I love you, but you fucking up right now.

Shit ain't right. Had your daddy done some shit like this to me, he

would have been dead."

"Ma, you don't even know who the fuck my daddy is. Stop

your shit why you in here trying to preach. I know the real you ma, and ummm you was a lil hoe out here." She couldn't do shit but laugh, because she knew I was telling the truth.

"Anyway, I love Raven. That girl been through a lot and she don't need your stanking ass adding to it. Get your shit together before I have to get involved. If I get involved, you know imma beat that ass."

"Aight Lady, I hear you." Getting up, I kissed her and headed home. I was not about to go back and forth with her talking about my business. When I pulled up, I took a deep breath. I had to remember Raven wasn't mine. I had a girl and she had a life outside of Chicago. When I walked in the door, Raven had on some sexy ass lingerie. When she started crawling towards me, my dick bricked up so hard, I forgot all about my girl. In the morning, we could say goodbye. As she wrapped her lips around my dick, I couldn't think about tomorrow. My head went back, and my knees buckled. I had no idea how I would ever let Raven go. Crazy thing is, San was mine, not her.

BE CAREFUL

SAN...

This nigga Rogue thinks I'm stupid. His ass been disappearing a lot lately and I'm supposed to just sit back and allow the shit to happen. When I question him on it, his ass says, he's with his friend. That bitch was on my last nerve and I know they fucking. Everything about him is different. When I curse his bitch ass out, he don't even get mad anymore. Bitch walking around happy as fuck.

Nigga don't even listen to rap no more. Mufucka riding around listening to 90's R and B. To make matters worse, I think the nigga sterile. After the first time he slipped up and forgot a condom, his ass made sure to use one every time after that. Shit didn't stop me because I was putting holes in his condom. Nothing was working, and I was getting frustrated. Jumping in my car, I drove to his warehouse. Yeah, I was doing a pop up, but I was on some sexy shit.

I had on a mini dress and some heels, minus the panties. I was about to fuck him silly over lunch and give him some fye head. Usually sex in a car is too spontaneous for a nigga to think about a condom. When I got there, I parked in the back, got out and walked in. If he was here by his self, I would fuck him all over the work and money. Usually, I would give him some head and get on about my business, but I needed to get pregnant and fast. When I got to the office, nobody was in there but Slim.

"Well, look at you coming in here ready to get fucked. A bitch pulls out all kind of tricks when they losing they nigga."
Ignoring the fact he called me a bitch, I wondered how he knew what was going on. Did Rogue tell him he was leaving me?

"I'm not about to lose shit. Where is Rogue?" This nigga started laughing and signaled for me to come here. When he saw I wasn't moving, he started back talking.

"Yeah, you definitely about to lose him. Oh, and this lil trick you trying to pull out your bag, she beat you to it. You don't have to believe me, I can show you better than I can tell you."

When he motioned for me to come over this time, I came. Pulling

me on his lap, I was uncomfortable as he started typing in some

shit on his keyboard. A video started playing and it showed Rogue

sitting at the desk counting money. His eyes kept closing and

finally his head fell all the way back. My worst fears came true,

when I saw Raven come from under the desk. When she mounted

him and started riding his dick, I knew he didn't put on a condom.

He could fuck this bitch raw, but not me.

This nigga Slim was watching and slightly moaning. His dick

got hard and I knew this hoe was turning him on as well. That shit

pissed me off. I was already betrayed by the man I loved, but this

bitch had everybody gone over her. What was it about this black

ass bitch that had these niggas forgetting what the fuck was

important? They ass was willing to risk it all over this hoe. Tired of

being outdone by this hoe, I started slowly grinding on his dick.

His shit was already brick hard, but once I started bouncing on it, I

thought the nigga was about to cum and his dick wasn't even out

of his pants.

97

He grabbed my titties rough as hell, but the friction was turning me on. I was gone need all the help I could get, because he wasn't all that cute and from what I felt, his dick wasn't big. This would be a piece of cake. Sliding off his lap, I unzipped his pants and pulled his dick out. Just as I thought, it was average. Licking my lips, I took all of him in and went crazy. That nigga was screaming like a bitch.

"Yeah what's up?" What the fuck, was that Rogue? Since he was the one saying what's up, Slim was the one that called him in there.

"Did you ummm… Did you count all the money?" I tried to get up, but he pushed my head up and down on his dick. Not wanting to create a scene, I just continued to suck.

"Don't I always? Is that all?" Slim laughed and I thought he was about to sell me out.

"Yeah, that's it. Close and lock my door on the way out. Oh naw, I need you to go swing by the trap and talk to B, his ass owes me some money and he been dodging me." I was glad he sent him away, how the fuck was I supposed to get out of here if he hadn't? I still wanted Rogue, I had too much invested. My heart and my time. This was payback and now we were even.

"Aight. I'll be back." I heard the door close and I came up from under the table.

"What the fuck Slim. That shit was foul as hell."

"Girl shut the fuck up. That was business, this is personal. Now come get personal." His ass was stroking his dick like he had a hammer. I was about to tell him no thanks, when I looked back at the screen. Slim had the shit still playing and the bitch was still riding my man's dick. Pulling my dress over my head, I climbed in his lap and put my titties in his mouth. As soon as he started sucking, he slammed me down on his dick.

I tried to take control, but his ass grabbed ahold of my ass and went to work. That shit wasn't that big, but it damn sure had some power. At least it wasn't a waste of my time. This payback sex was worth it like a mufucka. I mean, it wasn't Rogue, but it was definitely about to get this pussy off. His ass started moaning

99

and damn near screaming, ironically this time it turned me on. His ass wasn't thinking about Raven and in my mind, this was Rogue. Just the thought of him made me cum. In seconds, I was cumming all over his dick and he was lacing my walls with his kids. Climbing off him, I fixed my dress and got ready to leave. Even though me and Rogue was even, I still didn't feel good about the situation.

"Gone and put your number in my phone. I'll call you when I want some more of my pussy. That shit was fye and you got a good head on your shoulders too." This nigga had lost it. There was no way I was gone be out here having an affair with Rogue's boss.

"Naw, remember this pussy my nigga. It was a one time thing. It was good as fuck though." His ass started laughing and I knew it was gone be some bullshit.

"See, when a woman is emotional and angry, they don't think about shit that is right in their face. I just showed you a video of your nigga fucking another bitch. What does that tell you?" I looked at him like he was crazy, and then it hit me. This

100

nigga had cameras in here. Fuck. His bitch ass was blackmailing me into fucking him.

"Look, I just wanted to get even with Rogue. We did that. Let's not make this complicated, the shit was good. It is what it was, a fuck." He stood up with his average ass dick still hanging.

"It is, what I say it is. Let's not make this hard, because I don't want you to feel like you're being forced. We both enjoyed it and we're going to do it again. Look how wet that pussy is, shit running all down your legs. Now, put your number in my phone." Looking down, I did have some leakage. It wasn't because of him though, I just had that wet wet. It didn't matter whose dick went in that mufucka, this bitch was gone leak like a faucet. Not knowing if Rogue was gone continue to fuck that bitch or not, I said what the hell. We both could play this game. Grabbing his phone, I put my number in.

"Just know if we fucking, you paying. Let's not get this twisted, this pussy still checks a bag." He laughed, but I was dead ass serious. Since his dick was still out, I leaned down and sucked his shit one hard time. Instantly, his dick was brick hard. I released it and gave it a kiss. His ass was damn near shaking.

"You got it. Let's fuck one last time, you can't leave me hard like this." Now it was my turn to laugh. Walking towards the door, I looked back.

"You don't wanna overdose boo. Too much of this pussy will have you stalking a bitch. I gotta ration it to you, so we can keep this casual. This is not going to lead anywhere. Just two people fucking. Don't bitch up." Walking out the door, I eased out back and jumped in my car. Wiping my mouth I threw my shades on and turned on Cardi B's Be Careful.

SLIM...

Watching shorty leave only made my dick harder than what it was. Sitting down at my desk, I grabbed some oil and started caressing my shit. Looking at the video of Rogue and his lil side chick, I stroked my shit until my nut was about to come. That was until the door opened and Head walked in. Everybody thought I called him that because he was the leader of his crew,

but that wasn't it.

"Fuck is you in here doing my nigga?" I laughed and

motioned for him to come over.

"I was trying to get off, but you here now. Gone handle

this shit." Shaking his head, he walked over and glanced at the

screen.

"Why the fuck you looking at a video of Rogue fucking?

You want that nigga now?"

"Calm your ass down and do what the fuck I asked you. I

pulled it up for a reason. How many times I gotta tell you I'm not

gay? Fuck imma do with a nigga? Getting down on his knees, he

handled that for me and was done in five minutes. See, about five

years ago, Head owed me fifty thousand dollars. The nigga

couldn't pay me and begged me to do anything, so I wouldn't kill

him. When he started begging to suck my dick, I was about to put

a bullet in his head just from him fixing his mouth to ask me some

shit like that. My partner at the time stopped me and told me it would be the best thing I ever felt in my life. In the midst of us arguing about it, Head started stroking my shit and I was shocked when my dick got hard. I let him handle it, but that's as far as I would go. Head was head and that shit don't make you gay. If I crossed that line, then it was no going back.

I killed my partner that night, because his bitch ass jacked off as he watched the shit go down. I felt he would be a problem, and I eliminate all problems. Nigga also knew my secret, I would never allow a mufucka to blackmail me over some shit like that. Head got promoted and he sucks my dick whenever I want him to. San head was the best female I had, but nobody was touching him in that field. Looking over at this girl on tape, she looked like she might. Her technique was so fucking sexy, and you could see how wet her mouth was. Rogue had a big ass dick and she was making that mufucka disappear. I could only imagine what she could do with my shit.

"Nigga you staring at Rogue again. What is going on with you? I'm telling you now, you better not be fucking that nigga."

Punching his ass in the mouth, I shook my head at him. His ass was a clingy mufucka and I hated that shit.

"Stop questioning me like you my bitch. You serve one purpose, don't make me replace your bitch ass. I just took his bitch, but I'm starting to think that's not where his heart is. I need this bitch right here. Look how he looks at her." Head looked confused.

"Why you going after Rogue's chicks? Am I missing something?"

"Yeah, that nigga thinks he's bigger than me. Mufucka thinks he can talk to me reckless and I can't have that. His bitch was in here sucking my dick, while his ass was talking to me. You have no idea how that shit felt. I'm not sure that's the one that will hurt his soul though. I need her. After I take her, then imma kill his ass. Nobody on my crew is bigger than me." Glancing at the camera outside, I noticed he was sitting out there. Looking closer, I laughed. Getting up, I fixed my clothes and headed outside. Walking up to his car, I stood there and watched for a while.

"That pussy is talking. When you done Rogue, send her inside and let me sample that shit." The look that nigga gave me let me know he would kill over this bitch.

"Slim, shorty and Lady is the only two mufuckas on this earth that will make me put one in your head. Walk away before we have a problem." Smirking, I nodded and watched for a second longer. Heading back into the warehouse I realized, he didn't give a fuck about San. Since her pussy good, imma keep fucking her anyway. Shorty was the goal, I was gone get that bitch and make him watch while I fucked her. When I got back inside, I rubbed my hands together. The games were about to begin, and he had no idea. Rogue thought he was untouchable, but I was about to reach out and touch his ass. Grabbing my phone, I stored San's number.

"Hey nigga, why you on that creep shit? Is there a problem I don't know about, because we can straighten the shit out now? I don't have time to play blue's clues. What up?" This nigga was really starting to piss me off with his mouth.

"You seem to keep forgetting who the fuck is in charge. Watch your tone when you're talking to me. When there is a problem, you will know it." His ass had this shit fucked up.

"You're in charge of the streets nigga, not me. Don't forget that. You're just the nigga that signs the checks. The streets fear me, ain't nobody coming to see you Otis." This clown ass nigga walked out like what he said was law. Yeah, it was time for me to get rid of this bitch ass nigga. He out here thinking he me and shit. Anytime your crew start disrespecting you like this, it's time to put they ass to sleep. Rogue better count his fucking days. His shit was numbered.

INSECURE

RAVEN…

Opening the door at my mama's house, I wondered who the fuck it could be. Rogue had a key and Coi had gone back to Atlanta. When I opened the door, I was staring at some chick looking like she was ready to kill me. I'm assuming she had the wrong house, but she was mad as hell.

"Can I help you?" The girl scoffed and now I was really confused.

"You can start by staying the fuck away from my man. You think you can bring your black ugly ass back and just take him? Shit don't work like that. Look at me. Not only do I look better than your bucket ass, but I've held him down when you were somewhere fucking off." Taking a deep breath, I tried to calm myself down. She reminded me of those stuck up bitches in school. That thought that me being dark skinned made me ugly because they were light. Well, back then I was ugly, but it wasn't

108

because of my color. I hated mean girls and this bitch got me fucked up. Rogue is mine, always have been.

"I would advise you to get your hating ass off my porch. Being dark is beautiful but bitch I will get ugly real quick if you disrespect me again. I may be black, I may be ugly, but bitch I got hands. Try me."

"Look, I don't give a fuck about all of that. What kind of woman would fuck with a nigga knowing he has a girl? That's some desperate shit."

"Hello Barbara, this is Shirley." That hit a nerve on that hoe and I could tell she was ready to fight.

"Back up before you get smacked up. Fuck around and get your lil ass dragged out here." Coi came out of nowhere and I didn't even know she was back. Seeing that she had no win, she walked away.

"I'll be seeing you again Raven."

"I'll be waiting Barbara." Me and Coi walked inside and I couldn't help but laugh. I couldn't believe that bitch showed up to my door.

"I know her mama ain't named her no damn Barbara. Who is she? Don't matter, a dragged hoe was who she was about to be." My girl always showed up on time.

"That's Rogue's girl San. She came here on some woman to woman type shit. I guess my presence makes her insecure. Anyway bitch, why you here?"

"I wish I would have known that, I would have thrown that bitch in my car and drove her ass all the way home. Now, on to your dry pussy ass. What's taking you so long?"

"Fuck you mean? I've been doing everything you told me, and the shit been working. His ass is gone off me and we always together. I got a key to his shit and he got a key to mine." When she took a deep breath, I knew she wasn't impressed.

"All that sound good, but you don't have the nigga. He's fucking you and that bitch. All you did was give the nigga his cake and eat it too. Your ass supposed to be taking him away, not becoming the mistress. When you fucked him, you were only supposed to do it to get his ass sprung, then leave it dangling in the air. Not give him a key to it whenever he wanted it." Now I felt dumb as hell.

"You know I'm not into all these games and mind tricks. I just wanted him to myself. Maybe this is a fucked up plan. What if I do all this and he still don't leave her? Hell, he ain't left yet." Sitting down beside me, she grabbed my hand.

"That is always a possibility when they have a girl. I only helped you because you said it's what you wanted. You want reality, well here it is. If he does leave her, you may never trust him because he cheated so easily with you. He may actually love her and just a hoe ass nigga. You know the old Rogue, not this new one with money. Those niggas are different. You have to figure out what you're willing to take."

111

"See, I'm not bout this life. I just wanted the man I loved for all of my life. I didn't think about the consequences or the aftermath. What have I done? I fucked up Coi."

"No you didn't sis, you just got fucked. It's okay. He could possibly love you and want you too. Don't stress over it. I promise it will all work out."

"Naw bitch, that ain't what I mean. Yeah, I fucked up with that too, but I think I'm pregnant. The doctor can't see me until Tuesday and bitch it's Friday. I'm going to lose my mind waiting until then." This shit had become a mess and I had no idea what to do at this point if I became pregnant.

"Damn sis. Well look. Don't tell him until you know for a fact that you're pregnant. Put that shit all out on the table and if he doesn't leave her, then it's time for you to move on. Fuck him. It's other men out here besides Rogue ugly ass." I laughed, and the door opened.

"Hey Shorty." He looked so fucking fine and I swear it was going to be hard for me to walk away from him. I don't know how

I was going to do it, but I think I had to. This situation was messy

as hell and I didn't do mess. Coi got up to leave and walked past

Rogue like she was going to hit him. Placing her hand on his chest,

she rubbed her hand all the way down to his dick and gripped that

mufucka.

"Sorry, I told the hoe to send me a pic and she didn't

listen. Damn nigga that's a baby leg. Whew. I'm going to a hotel

sis, call me later." I dropped my head and shook it. Coi was crazy

as hell.

"Coi you touch my dick like that again, imma nut in your

nose. Stop playing with my man like that." She walked out, and he

came over and kissed me on the lips. It was time for me to be

strong and keep my pussy to myself. He was always someone

else's. I allowed my emotions to get the best of me and I went

where no woman should. "What's wrong Shorty?"

"Nothing. All we have been doing is fucking. Let's just hang

out tonight." He looked at me all weird and sat down.

"You know damn well we been doing more than fucking. I've taken you on more dates than I been on in my life. I've taken you shopping all kinds of shit. Do you understand, nobody has a key to my house, but you do?" I could tell he was getting frustrated, but hell, I was too.

"What are we doing? You have a whole girl and I'm out here fucking you like it's cool." This seemed to be a conversation he didn't want to have, and you could tell all by his demeanor.

"Shorty I don't know. Where is all this coming from? We been straight, let's not complicate this." Oh, he had me fucked up. It was already complicated.

"You right best friend. So, why are you in the drug game? You're so much smarter than that. Oh, and your boss, I don't trust him. Something about that nigga rubs me wrong. You have done great for yourself and I'm proud of you. Let me clean your money for you and we can walk away."

"I'm a street nigga Shorty. It's all I know. You want to talk, let's talk. How did you get all those scars on your body? What

114

happened?" This was a part of my past that I didn't like to talk

about. I just wanted to forget. Knowing he wouldn't let it go, I

decided to tell him.

"When I went to live with Coi and her mom, I got really

sick and found out I was pregnant. I called my mama asking her

for help and she shitted on my ass. Told me I wasn't her problem.

You were all I had and even you went missing in action. I felt

alone and worthless. Knowing I couldn't have that baby, I grabbed

a knife and started slicing my wrist. When I realized I would rather

be dead, I started stabbing myself. I didn't care where it landed, I

just continued to stab. Coi found me and they took me to the

hospital. I barely made it, but I did. I had lost everything, and I

didn't want to live no more. Those bastards took my life and got

away with the shit." The tears flowed from my eyes and Rogue

held me.

"You got me Shorty and they didn't get away with it. I

wasn't there to protect you then, but I got them baby girl. When

you told me what happened, I killed all they ass. I know it's not what you would have wanted me to do, but I did it because I couldn't bear the thought of them niggas walking another day not paying for that shit. I got you Shorty, always."

"Thank you, but you should have sent them to prison to get raped like they did me."

"You don't always have to go to jail to get raped. I had some big burly ass trans tear they ass from the rooter to the tooter." Looking up at him, I tried to see if he was for real. When I realized he was, I fell the fuck out.

"Did you really do that?"

"Yeah and if you really want me to walk away, I will do it for you." Just like that, my panties came down and I was Shirley again.

ROGUE...

Raven was fucking my head up and I had no idea what I was doing anymore. We were around here like a couple and I was scared to tell her how I felt. She had me doing shit I had never done before and the fucked up part is, I liked the shit. I would

have killed San if she had just popped up at my fucking house.

Raven ass been popping up everywhere, and all I did was try to

fuck because my dick be hard. She uses her key to my house

whenever she wants, and she shows up at the warehouse, just to

bring me lunch and shit. None of it bothered me, but I hated

when San did the shit.

What I was doing did not come easily to me. Every time I

looked in San's face, I felt like shit. Me and Raven haven't used a

condom yet, but I made sure to strap up with San. No matter how

fucked up the situation was, a nigga wasn't trying to have two

chicks pregnant at the same time. Hell, I didn't even want a baby,

but the thought of having one with Raven didn't sound bad. Right

now, she could pack up and leave with no warning. If she got

pregnant, I would always have ties to her.

Shit was all fucked up and this was what I was trying to

avoid. Yeah I fucked here and there, but none of those hoes

meant shit to me. I wasn't trying to play with no one's heart, now someone had to get hurt. How could I make a decision like this was beyond me. I owed San the world and she did her best to give me her all. Raven came in and stole my heart all over again like she did all those years ago. Do you walk away from true love because of obligation or do you say fuck the person that has had your back at your lowest, and follow your heart? San walked down the stairs and I could tell she had been crying.

"What's wrong San?" She sat down on the couch and just looked at me. "You good San?"

"Would you be good if a nigga from my past came back and stole my heart? How the hell can I be good, when you keep lying to me about this bitch calling her your friend?" I had no idea what she knew, so I wasn't about to say shit.

"San, she's just a friend. If I wanted her, I would be at her house and not yours." Usually, San just start yelling and I talk her down and we fuck. This time, she was crying, and I could see all the hurt in her face. It made me feel like shit.

"I don't know what I did to ever deserve the hurt you give, but I can't keep taking it Rogue. You had nothing, and I held you down. I've loved you and never cheated on you. All I asked for was your love. She comes in town and it was nothing for you to love her. You could have told me I wasn't enough, and I would have walked away years ago." My heart ripped, and I had never been more confused. San had been my rock for so long, I was fucked up for hurting her like this. I would have to just fight the feelings I had for Raven. Well, I would try my hardest.

"San straight up, I'm sorry. For all the bullshit I have done to you over the years. A nigga never meant to hurt you. Know that if you don't know shit else. Come here." Pulling her in my arms, I held her while she cried. "I love you San."

"I love you too Rogue. That's all I ever wanted, was for you to love me. I forgive you, but you can't be friends with her anymore. You know that right? Before you try to lie, I saw you with her. I came to the warehouse and there she was, riding my nigga's dick into the sunset." I refused to let her go and look her in the eyes. That is something I never wanted her to see, and I damn sure didn't want to get caught up with Raven, because I didn't want to let her go. I had my cake and I was eating it too. This shit just changed everything.

"I'm sorry San. I won't see her again. Well, I have to tell her face to face because she is my best friend, I owe her that. I'm all in." I guess me getting caught allowed me to make my choice.

"Ok. I'm going to take a shower. I'll cook dinner once I'm done." Nodding, I leaned my head back against the couch and closed my eyes. I don't know if I made the right decision, but it was too late to turn around now. I don't know how I was going to look Raven in the eyes when I told her this, but I owed her that. No more running. My phone went off and I looked at it.

Raven: Look how juicy your pussy is. I hope this makes your day a lil bit better.

Me: Why are you doing this to me. You know I can't come over tonight and you just gone torture me like this?

Raven: Why can't you cum? Don't I always make you cum.

My dick was busting out of my jeans and I swear I've never wanted anyone as bad as I wanted her right now. My shit was so hard, I was almost ready to jack off just to release. Looking at the video again, her shit sounded like mac and cheese. She was playing in her pussy and I knew I was about to fuck up. All that shit I had just told San, went out the window as soon as I saw this video.

Me: I'm on the way. Stay just like that.

Seeing the covers on the bed let me know she was at my shit. That's what I meant, even if I didn't come home, she would stay the night at my house just to feel close to me. When I would walk in the door, she wouldn't curse me out, she would just greet me with some head. Scrolling to San's name, I sent her a quick text.

SAN: Be right back. About to run to one of the traps. I'll be back in an hour, be cooking naked.

121

Grabbing my keys, I ran out the door and jumped in my car. My ass took off just in case she tried to come and stop me. I know I was fucking up and only making matters worse, but at least I could feel her one last time before I let her go. Pulling in my garage, I ran in the door and I was glad she was in the kitchen getting something to drink. Walking up behind her, I grabbed her by her hair and slammed her down on my island. Pulling my pants down, I released my hard ass dick. As soon as I slid it inside of her, it's like my shit exhaled. Knowing I didn't have time to waste, I pulled her head back and tore into her pussy.

Knowing it was my last time, I needed her to feel me all the way in her uterus. I was fucking her hard and fast. This nut was urgent, and I needed it. Her shit felt so good and tight on my shit and her screams made it worse. Not being able to hold it any longer, my shit shot out fast as hell inside of her. My body collapsed on top of her and I knew I had to get out of there.

"I love you Rogue. I'm not sure if you knew that already, but I do. I've loved you ever since I was old enough to know what that shit was. It's always been you and it will always be you."

Hearing her say that did something to me. I was no longer confused, I knew exactly what I had to do. It was about to be fucked up, but I had to let San go. All my life I loved and wanted this girl and never thought she could feel the same. To hear her say she was out here bad like my ass, let me know this shit wasn't by chance. This was some fate type shit. I didn't want to hurt San, I actually loved her too. Raven just had my heart.

"I love you too baby girl and you got me. I'm yours."

"Can you stay with me tonight?" I knew it was fucked up, but what else was I supposed to do.

"Yeah." Picking her up, I carried her upstairs. All the drama I was going to deal with would have to wait until tomorrow. Right now, I just wanted to be with my Shorty.

SURVIVAL

SAN...

It's been days since Rogue walked out of my house, talking about he was going to the trap. His ass got scared and ran like a pussy. I was tired of the back and forth with his ass, and I was ready to cut my losses. I refuse to be played like a dummy and on top of everything else, I been sick as hell. I was waiting on the locksmith to finish up, before I left to go to the ER. Rogue would not be able to come in and out of my house whenever he fucking felt like it.

Either he was going to do right by me or I was gone have to show him I didn't need his ass. Of course all of it was a big ass front and I was dying slowly inside, I couldn't help but wonder if he was with her. He sat his bitch ass right there and told me he chose me and then left like a fucking thief in the night. I couldn't believe that nigga had did me like that. When I came down the stairs and saw him gone, I grabbed my phone to call him. Seeing his text, I relaxed and started cooking. Naked, exactly like he

asked. After a few hours, I thought he got caught up. When I woke

up the next morning, he still hadn't come back. His ass wasn't

answering his phone or returning my calls. Here I was days later

and still no word from Rogue.

I was more hurt than anything. Every hour I changed my

mind about how I was going to handle him. One minute I was

done for good, the next I still wanted him, but needed him to

learn a lesson. I was confused as fuck, but one thing I was sure of

was, he had hurt me bad. I never thought this would be my life at

this point. He had fucked plenty bitches, but none of them

jeopardized my place in his life. My spot was always secure.

Now my dumb ass was over here wondering if I even still

had a nigga. Running upstairs, I threw up again and I couldn't wait

to get to the doctor. Rinsing my mouth out, I went back

downstairs and was happy to know the man was finished.

Grabbing my keys, I locked up and paid the man. Jumping in my

car, I headed to Jen's house. She was going with me to see what the fuck was going on. I needed someone there or my ass would lose it. When I pulled up, she was already outside waiting on me. As soon as she sat down, she looked over at me and started talking smack.

"Damn bitch, you look like shit. What the fuck is going on with you? I know you said you're sick, but damn." Rubbing my hand over my hair, I attempted to try and fix myself up. I know it wasn't gone help, but still.

"Rogue left." She looked unphased and confused.

"Girl, you and him don't live together. His ass always leaves and go home. Your ass always trying to be dramatic and shit. Where we going?" Rolling my eyes, I swear sometimes she could be so insensitive.

"No bitch. We were talking right, and I laid all of my feelings out on the line. He apologized for ever hurting me and he chose me. Told me he will stop being friends with Raven and all that good shit. I went upstairs to shower and when I came back, he was gone. I haven't heard from him since and that was days

126

ago. So, when I say he left. That's what the fuck I mean, he left." I was trying not to cry, but the tears came.

"That doesn't mean he is gone. Maybe he just needs time to tell her. He's never talked to you like that before, so maybe he just needs time to handle his business. Don't jump to conclusions friend. Y'all got too many years in this shit for him to walk away." I wanted to believe that, hell I needed to believe that. We drove the rest of the way in silence. When I pulled up to the hospital, we got out and I swear I wanted whatever drugs they were about to give me. Two hours later, I was sitting there looking at the doctor speechless.

"Pregnant?"

"Yes ma'am. About six weeks. I'll have them write up your discharge papers. Go see your primary, so you can get started on your prenatal care. Good luck." When she walked out, Jen looked excited as hell.

"Bitch you won. There is no way he is going to leave you and you're pregnant. Why the fuck aren't you looking happy about this. Am I missing something?" Fuck yeah she was. The whole damn problem.

"It's not Rogue's. Fuckkkk I can't believe this shit is happening to me." A bitch had to have the worse luck in history.

"Wait what."

"I found out he was fucking Raven and I slept with Slim. The nigga had it on tape, so he's been blackmailing me to fuck him. Me and Rogue only fucked once without a condom, and that shit was months ago. That nigga is going to kill me."

"Bitch no he's not. Listen, you just have to be smart. You tell the nigga you're pregnant and that's how you win. When you have the baby, act like that mufucka is late by a month. You got money, pay one of these doctors to change the date if he gets suspicious. Most niggas don't and have no idea what any of that shit means. You hold the cards now. Use it."

"How the fuck am I going to use it if he doesn't allow me to? That nigga is ghost and I have no idea where he's at. What I'm supposed to do, send the nigga a telegraph? A dancing baby to the warehouse." She laughed, but I was dead ass serious. Then I thought about it. "Bitch what about Slim? What if he wants the baby? He may tell Rogue if he sees me pregnant."

"Okay bitch. Why don't you tell Slim? See what he says and if he wants it, then choose that nigga. He got more money than Rogue anyway."

"Jen, me and Rogue have nothing to do with money. I love him, and this shit is all fucked up."

"You have to tell Slim, so you can see where his head is. If he wants it, he gone snitch on you anyway. At least if you with him, he won't let Rogue do shit to you." That made sense, but it wasn't the outcome I wanted. Regardless, I had to tell him.

"Okay, you're right. Pray for me bitch because this shit just became dangerous as fuck. All because this nigga wanted to fuck a bitch from his past. All this shit was Rogue's fault. I only slept with Slim to get back at him and now we were in a whirlwind of mess. This shit was all over the place and I don't know if I could fix it. I have no idea how Slim was going to respond and I wish I didn't have to tell his ass. If I knew whether or not he would rat me out, I wouldn't say a mufucking thing.

"Bitch I'm praying but drop me off at home. I want no parts of this shit. You gone have to tell me over the phone how this shit plays out. I didn't get dick from either one of they ass." Laughing, I headed towards her spot. I didn't blame her. Hell, I was a part of it, and even I didn't want to see how it played out. All I could do is pray that one of they asses fell for this raggedy ass plan. Shit could get ugly, but once she got out of the car, I headed to the warehouse to see Slim. If Rogue was there, I would just pretend I was there for him.

SLIM...

I had been following Rogue's girl for a few days now. Shorty was definitely not from the streets. She had no sense of street smarts. The girl not once looked behind her or glanced over her shoulder. Her happy ass just smiled and walked around as if everything in the world was peachy fucking cream. Not wanting to

130

approach her in a public place, I let her be. She had been staying

at Rogue's spot, so I couldn't approach her there either. Today

must be my lucky day, because she went to another house. Giving

it time to make sure she was staying, I went and tried the door

ten minutes later. Luckily for me, it was open.

When I didn't see her downstairs, I eased up to her

bedroom. Hearing the shower going, I sat on the bed and got

comfortable. I knew she was going to freak out when she saw me,

but she was gone have to get past that shit. Looking in her purse, I

saw her name was Raven. I heard the water stopped and waited

for her to walk out.

"OH MY GOD, what the fuck are you doing in my house?"

She was holding her towel tight as hell.

"You can quit acting like imma rape your ass. I don't take

pussy, you gone wanna give it to me. Fuck you doing with Rogue

anyway? Nigga got a whole girl and ain't going nowhere. I'm

single as fuck baby and my money way longer than his." You could

tell she was offended, but I didn't give a fuck.

131

"You sound childish and desperate as hell. What kind of nigga drags another nigga name to get some pussy? I'm not impressed." Standing up, it was funny to see she didn't flinch.

"Oh you should be very impressed. It's because of you that I haven't killed your nigga. I don't want to see someone like you hurt. This nigga you so impressed by, playing the shit out of you and San. He fucking both of y'all and leading both of you to believe he want you. You keep being impressed by that nigga though."

"Fuck you, how bout that."

"You will. Oh, and if you tell that nigga about this conversation, I will kill him. Come holla at me when you're done playing second to a bitch that ain't got shit on you." I could see her thinking and that was all that I wanted. It wasn't exactly how I wanted it to go, but the seed was set. I left out just as quietly as I came. Jumping back in my car, I headed towards the warehouse.

When I walked inside, I sat down stressed. I had Raven thinking, but if she told Rogue about our conversation, there was about to be a war. I wouldn't even see it coming if I didn't know

that she told him. I was gone have to make a move even though I

wasn't ready. I didn't quite think that shit through and now I may

have put a target on my head. Fuck.

"Can I talk to you?" Glancing at the door, San was standing

there looking a mess.

"Yeah what's up. For future references though, I don't do

the pop up shit. Just so we're clear on that.

"Look, I wouldn't have popped up if it wasn't important.

I've been sick, and I went to the doctor today. I'm pregnant."

"Shit, well come ride this dick then. You know they say

pregnant pussy the best pussy. That's the best revenge you can

have on that nigga, fucking me while you pregnant with his

shorty." She sighed, and I really wasn't in the mood for dramatics.

"The baby is yours Slim." Now that, I wasn't ready for.

"You can run that scheme on another nigga. You fucking

Rogue every day, how the fuck you want me to believe it's mine?"

"Because, he never fucks me without a condom. Is that good enough for you? I have no reason to lie, I'm about to lose everything." The way Raven and Rogue was carrying on, she already lost his ass. Maybe it's a way we could help each other. If Raven found out about the baby, there is no way she would stay loyal. The nigga was about to die anyway, she could use a shoulder.

"Naw, you not about to lose shit. As far as he knows, it's his. I don't do kids and like you said, it's just a fuck. Nothing serious. Everything will continue to go as it is. Stop worrying about that." You could tell she wasn't in the mood, but once I heard she had some pregnant pussy, I knew I was about to hit.

"Do we have to do this now, I really just want to go home and lay down?" Unbuttoning my pants, I pulled my dick out. That was her answer. I definitely needed some after seeing parts of Raven's chocolate ass body naked. Yeah she was wearing a towel, but she turned me all the way on. San walked over and locked the door. I went and sat on my couch. Texting Head, I told him to

134

come in my office. When he came in, I couldn't quite read what was going through her mind.

"Lock the door." Head did what I told him, and you could tell he was turned on, but I didn't know how San was going to feel about this. Attempting to get my dick sucked and keep my secret, I tried something different. Motioning for San to come to me, I leaned my head back against the couch. "Come ride my face." She pulled her clothes off and climbed on with no problem. Head knew what to do from that point on. His mouth hit my dick instantly. I sucked the shit out of San's clit while Head got me brick hard.

I was eating that pussy so good, San didn't even attempt to look back and see that Head was swallowing my shit. When she came in my mouth, I pushed Head out the way and slid her down to my dick. Shorty went crazy. It seemed as if she thought Head was in here to fuck her as well. They said most girl fantasies was to have two guys at the same time, so I gave her what she wanted.

135

"I think she want some dick in her mouth Head." When she leaned her head back and opened her mouth, that shit turned me all the way on. I had to focus hard as hell, so I wouldn't cum. He came over and put his dick in her mouth and she started sucking hard while bouncing that ass on me. As soon as he was hard, he pulled out and pushed her down. Grabbing her by the ass, he lifted her enough to slide his dick in.

She screamed out, but that only turned everyone on. We both started tearing her up at the same time. When I felt head grab my balls and massage them at the same time I was all in that pussy, I had to kiss San to avoid screaming out like a lil bitch. I came hard and there was no way my shit was getting back up. Stopping them, I let her climb off me and I moved out the way. My dick was too tender to be trying to fuck soft. Head pushed her on the couch and slid inside her pussy and fucked her from behind.

If that was my bitch, I would have been jealous. That nigga was tearing her shit up and she was loving every bit of it. His dick

136

was soaked from pussy juices. San got wet, but she ain't never drenched my shit like that. They were going at it and the shit was entertaining as hell to watch. When he came, that nigga shook the entire couch. San was screaming and shaking, and my dick was back hard as hell. After the round they just went, I knew there was no way she was letting another dick up in her again. Barely getting up, she fixed her clothes and walked out. All I could do was shake my head.

If I was a real nigga, I would cuff the bitch and make her mine. Laughing at myself, I looked over at Head and nodded towards my dick. He locked the door and walked over to me. That shit was back standing up and I needed it relieved. Leaning my head back, I closed my eyes and waited for his mouth to hit my shit.

When I felt him slide down on my dick, I knew he had just crossed me over to the point of no return. His ass felt better than any pussy I had ever felt in my life. I wanted to kill him and fuck him at the same time. I wasn't gay, but it was too late, and I was

about to give in to the one thing I swore I would never do.

BABY MAMA DRAMA

ROGUE...

I had been dodging the fuck out of San because I really didn't know what to say to her. I couldn't bring myself to see the look of hurt on her face. We had so many years invested, there was no way out of this without me fucking her up. As messed up as it was, I knew where I was supposed to be. It didn't make the shit any easier though. All I wanted was to make Raven happy, but in order to do that, I had to hurt San.

She didn't deserve what I was about to do to her and that is what bothered me the most. Yeah she nagged and shit, but she was down and loyal as fuck. Here I was trying my best to get Raven pregnant and San had been begging me for years to have a baby. I was fucked up on so many levels, I couldn't look her in the face. Knowing I owed it to her, I stopped by Lady house to see if she could give me a way to do this shit. An easy way.

139

Walking in her house, I looked at her sitting on the couch without a care in the world. She was sipping wine and laughing at something on the TV. I knew she was about to light my ass up, but at this point, I didn't even give a fuck. I needed help and I was gone have to take it in order to figure out what the fuck to do. Sitting down, I grabbed a blunt out of my pocket and started rolling it.

"What up Lady?" She just stared at me. Grabbing the remote, she turned the Tv off and started sipping her wine as she stared at me.

"Don't get quiet now with your dumb ass. What did you do? It's the only time you smoke with me, when it's something serious." All I could do was lick the blunt and shake my head. She knew me well.

"I fucked up bad Lady and before you say anything, I already know you was right. We can skip that part of the talk. Me and San had a talk and she poured her heart out to me. I told her I would do right by her and leave Raven alone. I chose her, but as

140

soon as Raven texted me, I was out the door and over there professing my damn love to her. The thing is Lady, I meant every word. I love the shit out of that girl and she makes me wanna be better. I just don't know how to be happy, without hurting San." Lady looked at me and grabbed the blunt. Lighting it, she took a long ass pull and looked at me.

"Yeah son. You fucked up. I'm not even sure how you could fix it at this point. You're gonna have to tell her the truth no matter how bad it hurts her. Women are resilient. We go through so much in a lifetime, but we always seem to pick up the pieces and keep pushing on. I never understood why we were the most disrespected. We make a life, carry it, and birth it. That pain alone is like no other. We go through heartache, disrespect on the job, looked over for promotions because they gave it to some undeserving ass nigga. Come home, clean, cook, and bathe the kids. Doing all this shit alone, with the weight of the world on our shoulders. No matter what we go through, we cry, get up, and keep going. You know why son? Because if we don't, no one else would." This mufucka then went into a life lesson on women and all I wanted to know was what the hell to do.

"Ma, I get that. The damage is already done, and I fucked up. Now what am I supposed to do?" She shrugged her shoulders.

"Tell her the truth son. How did you not get what I was saying? She will be okay. It will hurt like hell at first, but she will pick up and move on eventually. Give her that freedom though. If you don't tell her, she will continue to find a way to fight for you and that's not fair to her." Dropping my head, I knew she was right. She deserved to know my decision.

"How the hell did you get so smart?"

"Nigga I'm not smart. I got played all my life by fuck niggas." Lady was crazy as hell.

"You had a good life with pops. Your entire life wasn't dealing with fuck niggas ma."

"Lies you tell. Your daddy took me through hell. It was that tenacity, the resilience I'm telling you about that kept me going. We were finally happy, and I can say that I found my soul mate.

When he died, I knew I wouldn't get that again. I'm okay with that, it took too long to get that nigga to act right." I laughed on the outside, but that still bothered me. My pops died while I was in jail. That shit hurt like a mufucka.

"Ma, why you always talking shit? I came over here trying to bond and get some help from you, and your ass in here playing."

"I'm not playing. That lil corn on the cob put in work. His ass stayed cheating." Now I was lost.

"What the hell is a corn on the cob?" She took another sip of her wine and leaned forward.

"Son, that nigga had a bumpy piece of meat. I swear the first time he pulled it out, I thought the nigga had that clap on clap off. I made his ass go to the doctor, but they said he was clear. That it was normal. So, I started calling that nigga corn on the cob." Nope, I wasn't about to do this shit.

"That's my cue. You sure know how to ruin some shit. Here we were having a great conversation and your ass wanna bring up another nigga's meat. I'll be back to see you and tell you how it went."

"Your ass always dumping your problems on me, but I can't tell you what the fuck I be going through. You want to sit here and tell me how you fucking two bitches, but I can't tell you my vibrator no longer works. It died on me. Fuck you, your ass selfish." Laughing, I leaned down to give her a kiss.

"You know I love you Lady. I just would rather not know certain shit about you. I'll be back. Call me if you need anything."

"You know I don't want that dirty ass money. Talk to you later." Leaving out, I was heading to my house, when Raven called me.

"What up Shorty, you at my crib?"

"No, I had an appointment, I'll be back in a few. I just wanted to check on you and make sure you're okay." She sounded worried and I had no idea why. I was good out here in these streets, but none of that mattered. I was about to walk away, and she knew that.

144

"I'm good. I told you not to worry about me. Your nigga not some lil pussy ass mufucka. Just hurry up and bring that ass home."

"Okay, I love you."

"Love you too Shorty." Hanging up, I called San, but she didn't answer. Shooting her a quick text, I let her know we needed to talk. When I pulled up to my house, I noticed San was on my porch. Pulling into the garage, I went inside and walked to the front opening the door. San walked in and I knew this was not about to go well.

"Let's just cut through the chase. I'm pregnant Rogue."

RAVEN...

Looking over at Coi, I was sitting nervously waiting on the doctor to come in the room. I was pretty sure I was pregnant, but I had no idea how Rogue would take it. He's never talked about wanting kids, only how San always tried to push him into having some. This may be something he didn't want, and I had no idea if this was going to tear us apart. He could be happy as hell about it, but that was just it. I didn't know what to expect. We had been doing so good, and I could be about to ruin that. They said nothing worth having comes easy. Coi could tell I was nervous, and she grabbed my hand. She knew what I went through the last time I was pregnant, and she just wanted to make sure I was good. The doctor walked in and I held my breath.

"Yes, you are definitely pregnant. Around three months. You're going to be a mommy, congratulations." Smiling I told her thank you. She went over the rest of my test and let me know to see my regular doctor. When she walked out of the room, I looked at Coi.

"Okay bitch, she gone now put that pussy up. I'm a freak, but I don't do coochie cat. How are you feeling?" I Laughed as I got dressed.

"I'm happy for the first time in my life, but I'm nervous as hell. I don't know how Rogue will take it. We've come so far and now, I could be setting us back. Bitch, should I tell him or wait?"

"You have to tell him dummy. He deserves to know. You all will be fine, trust me. He loves you and I'm sure he will want the baby. Bitch I'm ready to cry this is one hell of a love story. I can't believe you did it. You got your soul mate."

"Your ass better be right or I'm blaming you. All this shit was your idea and if I walk away hurt, I'm beating your ass and you the damn daddy." We laughed and headed out.

"I'll be the pappy, I don't give two fucks. The baby is going to be good no matter what. Just have a little faith. Now let's go tell your man the good news." I love the support her and her mother has always given.

"Thank you sis, for everything. But your ass can't come with me. I'll call and tell you the news when it's over. This is a moment for just us."

"Whatever bitch, drop me off then. Petty ass." Laughing, I took her to my house. When she got out, I called Rogue and let him know that I was on the way. He sounded so happy and that gave me the strength I needed to tell him. It would be okay, and I knew that now. We were destined to be together and it was meant for us to have this baby. When I got to his house, I pulled in the garage and parked next to his car. Since I had been here, he let me drive his truck and that shit came in handy. I had been here a while which meant I would have been paying for a rental all this time. Using my key, I walked in the house. What I didn't expect was to find him and San sitting on the couch talking. When he saw me, he jumped up and I could tell shit wasn't about to go as smoothly as I thought.

"This bitch got a key to your house? We've been together for years and I can't even get a panty drawer, but this hoe got a key." I was so over this chick's dramatics.

"Refrain from addressing me by any other name other than Raven. Your issue is with him, not me. Don't get your ass whooped in here."

"I'll call you whatever the fuck I want. You not gone do shit but stand your black ass over there and look ugly. Stupid bitch. Rogue, this what we doing?" When I took off running towards her,

148

Rogue grabbed me. That shit pissed me off. Looking at him, I couldn't believe he was protecting her.

"I can't let you do that Raven. She's carrying my shorty." I paid close attention to how he called me by name and her baby was now Shorty.

"Yeah bitch. I'm carrying his child. We will never be over, get that through your head." I waited for him to correct her and tell them they been done, but his ass just stood there looking stupid.

"Well then. I guess I'm done here, and I'll let you two get back to what you were doing. I'm sorry I interrupted you." Throwing his keys on the counter, I walked out the door and grabbed my phone. Coi picked up on the first ring.

"Come get me."

"I'm on the way." She knew the tone of my voice and I didn't have to explain anything. Rogue came running outside and I swear I never hated him more than I did right now.

"Raven, I'm sorry. I didn't know she would be here. She came to tell me that she was pregnant. I didn't mean to hurt you. Please don't be mad at a nigga." I laughed and clapped my hands.

"You never meant to hurt me? What the fuck did you think was going to happen and you were fucking us both at the same time. You should have never took it there with me. I was your best friend and you couldn't even man up and be honest." His jaw line was jumping, so I knew I hit a nerve.

"Honest. Let's be honest. The first time we fucked, you knew I had a girl. You climbed in the shower with me. I didn't ask you to do that. I almost lost everything for you. I was willing to give up everything for you, but I can't walk away from my child Raven. I'm not built like that."

"A child I could deal with, but that's not what you're saying. You can't walk away from her since she's carrying your child. I'm good with that, have a nice life." When he didn't tell me I was wrong, I couldn't stop the tears that fell from my eyes. Raising my hand, I slapped the shit out of him. "Fuck you Rogue."

150

Walking off, I left out his gate and waited for Coi at the curb. They can have each other, and I was taking myself out the game. Yeah I could have told him I was pregnant, but that's not how I wanted him to choose me. I wanted him to pick me because his heart told him too. I looked back one last time and he wasn't even standing there. His ass had gone back inside, and I pictured them hugging as he rubbed her stomach. My body started shaking and I felt like I was about to pass out. My legs got weak and right as I got ready to fold, I felt arms around me. Coi had caught me and just like any other time in my life, she was right there when I needed her. She put me in the car and as soon as the door closed, I broke down.

"Why don't he want me? Sis, how could he do me like this? I loved him, and he was supposed to love me. Get me out of here and take me home."

"I got you sis. We'll be there in no time. We can order some food and drink. Well, you can watch me drink."

"No, take me home. To Atlanta. There is nothing for me here. I don't need anything there, just get me the fuck out of here. Fuck him and fuck Chicago." You could tell Coi didn't agree with that, but I didn't care.

"What happened?" After I explained everything to her, she was crying with me. "You not gone tell him about the baby?"

"No, he has a family. Like you said, you'll be the daddy. Take me home." Nodding her head, she drove towards the airport. Balling up as much as I could in the seat, I cried the entire time there. My phone went off and I looked down to see it was Rogue.

Rogue: I'm sorry.

Not even responding, I blocked him from my phone and from my life. I was never coming back to this raggedy ass city. It has brought me nothing but heartache.

NEXT LIFETIME

ROGUE...

This shit did not go down how I expected it to go, but what was I supposed to do? There was no way I could leave San and she was pregnant with my child. That shit would be fucked up on so many levels. I wouldn't even want a woman who was okay with me saying fuck my shorty. The last thing I wanted to do was hurt Raven, hell I didn't want to hurt anybody, but the shit went all wrong. Even though I told San she could stay with me, I needed some space for a moment. The girl I loved just walked out of my life and she didn't want anything else to do with me.

"I'll be back. I need a minute."

"You don't have to feel bad about choosing your family. That's what a real nigga does. I love you and I can't wait for the baby to get here."

"I know San. I just need some time to myself. You don't have to worry, she wants nothing to do with me. I'll be back."

Grabbing my keys, I jumped in my truck and drove off. I could still smell her inside. Her perfume was stuck in my leather or something. Whatever it was, I was happy it was there. Driving to her house, I went to apologize one more time. Getting out of my car, I used my key to get in.

Walking around, I realized she wasn't there. Climbing in her bed, I thought about what I had lost. She came into my life at the wrong time and it just wasn't meant to be. Maybe we could be together in another life, but right now, it just wasn't meant. I had laid there so long, I didn't realize a few hours had passed. Getting up, I walked downstairs and outside.

"What the fuck you done did now? You look like shit. Matter fact, you look like the shit I just took a lil while ago. What the hell is wrong with you? San didn't take it well?" Lady was out there screaming at me talking shit in her normal fashion.

"Naw, San at my house. It's Raven that I hurt." Lady looked confused and I understood why. The last time I was here, I told her I was in love with Raven and I had chosen her. Now I was saying San was at my house. I had really made a mess of things and I wish I could take it all back.

"She's pregnant, I couldn't leave her. I know what I told you and I meant every word, but I can't walk away from my family."

"I don't know what the hell going on, but I'm gone let you handle it. Just know son, you could be a father without sacrificing your heart. I'm just gone pray for everybody involved, because all y'all got fucked over. SON MOVE." Out of nowhere, Lady jumped in front of me as shots rang out. We fell to the ground and she was on top of me with a death grip. I tried hard as hell to get her up, but she wasn't going. When the shots stop, she finally released me and rolled over.

"Lady why the fuck would you do that?" She was bleeding, so I knew she jumped in front of a bullet for me.

"Because I'm your mother. If I die, you have to get your life right or all of this was for nothing. No more streets, I need you to let it all go." Tears fell from my eyes and I held her tight. She was

155

my everything and I can't believe someone was dumb enough to shoot at me.

"Ma, please don't leave me. You're my sanity in this crazy ass world. Imma get you to the hospital, just hang in there for me. I got you and I'll walk away. If God save you, I'll walk the fuck away." Picking her up, my body shook as I tried to carry her. Not because she was heavy, but because it felt as if I was losing everything.

"Son, I'm okay." Her voice was low, and I just needed to get her to the hospital.

"I got you ma. You don't have to be strong right now. Let me be that for you.

"No, for real. I'm okay. It was just my shoulder. I can walk nigga put me down." Looking at her and seeing she was serious, I wanted to slap the shit out of Lady ass. Letting her go, I let her ass hit the ground. "That was fucked up son, after I just poured my heart out to you. You ain't shit"

156

"I should make your ass walk to the hospital. I see you think this shit a joke, but you almost got the whole city murdered. Don't scare me like that no more." She laughed, but I didn't find shit funny. Putting her in my truck, I drove her to the hospital.

"Son, if you chose San, why were you at Raven's house?" Taking a deep breath, I knew she was about to go off.

"I wanted to talk to her. You know, try to explain the situation. She walked in when San had just told me, so I may not have handled it right." I wasn't expecting for her to slap me. This was the second time a woman had hit me, and I couldn't do shit about it.

"Who the fuck raised you? How many times you want to tell the girl you not choosing her? Leave her alone and let her heal. Your dumb ass wanna keep bringing it up to her like that's going to help. I said the hoe resilient not super woman. That shit hurts. Hurry up and take me to the hospital before I be done beat your ass in this car."

"Ma, you two seconds away from walking."

157

"And you two seconds away from looking like Iron Man. Drive nigga before I beat your ass." Shaking my head, I headed towards the County. When we got there, I dropped her off.

"I'll be back. I need to go find out what the fuck is going on. It's time to make some shit shake." When she looked at me, I knew what she was about to say.

"Shoot they dick in the dirt when you catch them. This shit hurts like hell." That damn sure was not what I thought she was gone say. "What? don't look at me like that. What's the point in having a son in the streets if he can't kill a nigga for shooting his mama? I don't want you out there, but I'm not a punk bitch. Don't take all day either, I'm hungry and I don't want no baby food and crackers." Shaking my head, I nodded at Lady then tore ass towards the warehouse. If we were at war, I should have been notified.

When I pulled up, nothing seemed to be going on. Even when I walked inside, everyone was going on about their day as if nothing was going on. That shit rubbed me as odd. I stood there and waited to see if anyone was going to say anything, but

mufuckas just kept counting money and bagging up work.

"Meeting in five minutes. Anybody not here, have to

answer to me." They looked up and everyone looked confused.

"Aight boss man, you got it." Sending a quick text to Slim, I

made sure he knew about the meeting, so his bitch ass could be

there. Somebody knew something, and I needed to know what

the fuck is going on. As soon as Slim came in, I got started.

"Somebody was dumb enough to shoot at me like it was

sweet. They hit my mama and the city gotta feel me behind that

shit. Now, was there a beef or war that I wasn't made aware of?

because if so, we have a mother fucking problem and y'all gotta

see me." Everyone sat there quiet and it was pissing me off.

"SPEAK." Looking over at Slim, I really didn't like the fact that he

didn't speak up.

"Boss man, I don't know shit about a beef. This shit new to

me as well, but you can believe imma hit those streets to find out

who violated. I got you." Geno was loyal as fuck and I liked that in

159

him. His ass wasn't afraid to speak up and didn't break his neck to kiss Slim's ass. He was like me.

"Did you not hear Rogue ask a mufucking question? Somebody knows something and if you don't, speak the fuck up and say you don't. His mother was hit and you niggas sitting here like that shit ain't urgent. Will the shit become urgent if we start fading you niggas?" Slim had stood up and went the fuck off. He was lucky he did that shit, because I was looking at him real funny up until that point. Everyone started speaking up saying they ain't know shit and this wasn't adding up.

"Well that means, someone out there wants a war, but a dirt box is what they gone get. Hit the streets and find out who the goofy was and I'll take it from there." When I left out, something was eating at me, but I couldn't figure it out.

RAVEN...

It took everything for me to climb out of the bed. I had been lying here for a month, only getting up to eat and wash my

RIGHT AND A WRONG WAY TO LOVE A DOPEBOY

ass. It's not that I didn't try to get out of my funk, the shit was just

hard. The baby had me sick as hell and I had fallen into a deep

depression. I wouldn't even answer the phone for even Coi. I just

wanted to be alone.

In my mind, I had gone through my rape all over again.

This time, by someone I loved. Rogue raped me of my heart, my

trust, and my loyalty. Now, I was sitting here carrying his baby.

While he was choosing to be a family with that bitch, I was stuck

here to raise my baby on my own. My heart was hurting, and it

was taking over my thought process. Grabbing my phone, I looked

up a number.

"Hello, I was wondering if I could make an appointment to

come in."

"Yes you can. What is your name and date of birth?" After

giving it to her, she asked more questions. "How far along are

you?" This was the tricky part. I hoped this was one of those

clinics that wouldn't deny me because I was five months. All of

them wouldn't do it.

"I'm five months. Will that be a problem?" When she got quiet, I knew she was judging, but I didn't give a fuck.

"No, it's not a problem. It will cost more though, is that okay with you?"

"That's fine. Money is not an issue."

"We have an opening for tomorrow, if that is not too soon." I wanted to get this done as soon as possible.

"That's fine." After hanging up, I laid down and cried. If I had waited any longer, I would definitely change my mind. This wasn't a decision I came by lightly, but it had to be done. This baby would be a constant reminder of the hate I had for Rogue. I couldn't bring myself to do that to my child. The hurt was too grave, and I had to release all ties from him. Closing my eyes, I drifted back off to sleep.

Feeling my pussy throbbing, I opened my eyes to find Rogue between my legs sucking on my pussy. As much as I wanted him to stop, my body wouldn't let me. The feeling was too intense. I tried to get him to stop, because this was wrong.

162

"Please no. We can't do this. You hurt me, and I have to let you go. I can't keep allowing you to come in and out of my life. That shit hurt." Coming up from my pussy, he said shh against my lips.

"I hurt you, now let me make you feel good. Let me take your pain away. I need you. Shorty, I need to feel you." He spread my legs and I couldn't do shit but let him in. My body was craving him, and I needed him inside of me. As soon as the tip broke through, I screamed out. It filled me up and it took my breath away. "Fuck, I missed you so much Shorty. Tell me this pussy will always be mine."

"It's yours Rogue. It will always be yours." His pace picked up and he went in deeper.

"Tell me you not gone give my pussy away." Screaming as loud as my tonsils will let me, I had to gather my thoughts in order to say the words.

"I'll never give it away. Fuck, I'm about to cum."

163

"Me too Shorty." Leaning down, he kissed me as he slammed into my pussy. Our bodies were in sync and we came hard together.

"I love you Rogue." I waited for him to say it back, but he just stared at me.

"Raven, what the fuck are you in here doing? Your ass screaming like somebody killing your ass. Look at my sheets. Your ass better not be in here on no freaky shit bitch." Opening my eyes, I realized it was all a fucking dream. Coi was looking at me like I was crazy and shit. It was morning and I glanced at the clock. It was time for me to go to my appointment.

"I'm good, I gotta get up and go to the doctor. I'll call you later."

"You tried it, I'm going with you. I'll be in my room getting dressed." She walked out, and I had to look between my legs to see if I was tripping. My pussy was still throbbing and leaking juices. The shit felt so real and you couldn't have paid me to believe Rogue wasn't here. I jumped in the shower fast as hell,

164

because I didn't want Coi to go with me. This was going to be a five minute cleaning, because I needed to be gone before she got ready. Paying real close attention to my pussy area, I cleaned the shit out of that mufucka and got out. My door was open, so I knew this bitch came to check and see if I was ready.

Quietly, I got dressed, grabbed my purse and snuck out. I had been staying at her house, because she wanted to keep an eye on me. Last time I was this depressed, I tried to kill myself and I guess she said not on her watch. Sliding in my Infinity truck, I took off and headed to the clinic. Coi started calling my phone, but I hit decline and turned up Eryka Badu's Next Lifetime. I guess it just wasn't meant to be for me and Rogue and I had to accept that. I needed to erase all ties to him and this was the only way to do that.

When I got there, they took me in the back and got me set up. I was waiting on the anesthesiologist to come and give me general anesthesia for the abortion. Waiting on them to come in, had my nerves on edge. Would Rogue care? Would he be pissed?

165

Was I making the wrong decision based off emotion? I felt so selfish and I couldn't believe I was about to get rid of my baby over a nigga. Panic started to set in and all I could do was cry. What was going on with me?

God, in the past it has always felt like you abandoned me. I need you now, more than I ever have. There is a life in my hands and I don't want to make the wrong decision. I know I'm not your most favorite person. You have allowed a lot of pain and hurt in my life. I try to stay faithful and believe, but it's hard when everything in my life is tearing me down. How could one person be so unloved? How could so much pain be inflicted on one person? This is not about me though. It's about an innocent child and I need your guidance. I need you to for once hear my cries. Please God tell me what to do. I need to know what to do.

I prayed my heart out and nothing happened. I don't know what I did to God, but it felt as if he hated my entire existence. I needed him, and he was nowhere to be found, yet again. My heart bled out right on the table and I cried like I never have before. Everyone always abandoned me, and my heart couldn't take no more.

"I don't give a fuck if she didn't okay me to be back here, I'm going. Who gone stop me. Get your ass up off this damn table. I wish the fuck you would kill a baby. THAT IS A BABY. Not a blood clot, not a toy, not a pawn in you and Rogue's shit. Get your ass up before I drag you off this table."

"Ms. Woods, would you like for us to call the police and have her escorted out?" Sitting up, I looked at Coi and up at the sky. For once, he didn't abandon me.

"Naw, but you can give me a minute to get dressed. I won't be going through with the procedure." The nurse actually smiled, and I felt good about my decision. It was as if a peaceful breeze went over my body. After I got dressed, she grabbed my hand and we walked out together.

"Don't think you out of the woods, I told my mama." There was Auntie Cheryl standing there waiting for me. I was wrong, I was not alone. They have always had my back and today was no different. I smiled at her and she looked at me with the fakest grin ever.

"Bring your dumb ass on before I whoop your ass in here. Got us in here showing our ass in front of these white people. Why this bitch at my house?" Me and Coi fell out at her copying Monique in Precious.

"I'm sorry auntie, please don't whoop me."

"I know you're hurting, and you have caught a bad break in life, but we got you. Don't you ever forget that."

"I know, and I love y'all." The tears fell again, but this time, it didn't hurt so bad.

NO SHAME

SAN...

"Naw bitch, we didn't think this shit all the way through. You told me this shit would balance itself out, but I can't make this shit add up. I'm supposed to be eight months, but I'm only five. My stomach nowhere near looks like I'm ready to give birth." Jen was looking at me like this wasn't her dumb ass plan.

"Girl, I didn't tell you the shit would work the entire way. It was to get you to win the nigga. You did that, the rest on your ass. You better act like the baby premature or something." I looked at this hoe like she was crazy.

"Bitch, it's time for the baby shower and I'm just now about to find out what the hell I'm having. My stomach little as hell and Rogue ain't no dummy. Maybe I need to see if they will abort the baby and I tell they ass I lost it." She shook her head at me like she was disgusted.

"You gone kill your baby over a nigga? That shit pathetic. Grow the fuck up. You messed up, either you ride the lie out until you can't no more or tell them the truth. Niggas not that smart when it comes to babies. His ass ain't been to that many of the appointments because you always schedule them around the times he can't. Be smart mufucka or give up." This hoe was going hard like I wanted to be in this shit.

"Don't do the most. Yeah, I fucked up, but I'm trying to figure out a way to fix your dumb ass plan. Shit, it's not no easy fix."

"You right bitch, it ain't. I'm glad I'm not in your shoes. My timing for my pregnancies be close. I always fuck my niggas together bitch. Your ass shouldn't have listened to me no way, I don't know." We both laughed at the mess I was in, when Rogue walked in the house. He mugged me so hard, I knew it was going to be a fight tonight.

"Tell your company goodnight San." My ass was embarrassed at how he treated her.

170

"Damn nigga, you act like can't nobody come in your funky ass house." I was trying to shake my head at Jen, but she wasn't paying me any attention.

"I don't think I was talking to you, but I can just tell you to get the fuck out. San knows I don't do company." Mouthing I'm sorry to her, I got up to walk her to the door.

"He don't trust people. I thought you would be gone before he got back. My bad bitch."

"I'm confused, it's your house too. Fuck that, you better put your foot down."

"Bitch bye, that same foot gone be in my mouth if I don't figure out how to get out this mess." Waving, she left, and I walked back inside. My text went off and I thought it was her, but it wasn't.

773-792-7742: Come to the warehouse

That was all it said, so I knew who it was. Looking over at Rogue, I didn't know how this was going to play out. His ass was in a bad mood and I could use that to get away. Hopefully.

"I'm going over to Jen's house since you don't want her here. We were having girl's night and I need that right now. I'm pregnant and emotional, and your ass never here." Rogue looked unmoved.

"Seems to me you have a lot of girl's nights. Your ass always gone and shit ain't adding up. Play with it if you want to, but don't outgrow your brain. Shit won't work out for you."

"Fuck are you talking about? You can be gone all day and night and I can't question you on shit, but the minute I leave, it's a problem. I'm not slow, I'll be back later." Rolling my eyes, I walked out to my car. This nigga was starting to text me more and more to roll through and I couldn't keep lying about my whereabouts. The crazy thing is, the shit was fye as hell. Especially since me and Rogue barely fucked. Crazy thing is, the nigga still wore a condom every time.

When I got there, I parked around back and walked inside. Head was sitting in the office waiting on me. I ran into him at the store one day and next thing I knew, we were fucking in the back of his truck. Slim didn't really call me up anymore to hit, but I've

been giving it to Head on the regular. That nigga had some good

big dick and my ass was getting sprung on that shit. Of course, I

didn't want his ass, but man it was gone be hard to let that dick

go. Once I had the baby, I was gone stop my shit and be faithful to

Rogue. Right now, I was still getting even and having fun doing it.

"Get over here and suck this dick." Walking over to the

chair he was sitting in, I got down and took him in my mouth. The

best thing about him, was he never wanted head long. After

sucking it enough to get it hard, he grabbed me by my hair and

pulled me up. Kissing me, he shoved his tongue in my mouth and

sucked on my tongue. No matter what, he always sucked my

tongue like his life depended on it. Turning me around by my hair,

he slammed me on the desk. Spreading my ass, he slid inside of it.

No matter how much we did anal, that shit always felt like

he was ripping me open. His dick was humongous, but it felt so

good. Pulling my head back, he started hitting this shit from the

back. Using his other hand, he massaged my pussy and my shit

173

was soaking wet. Pulling out of my ass, he dropped down and started sucking my asshole. That was half the reason I was gone off his sex, this mufucka was nasty. There was no way Rogue would ever do half the shit Head does. I loved that nasty shit and I always came hard as hell. Rising back up, he slid in my pussy and started fucking. I knew that shit wasn't right, but again, I loved that nasty shit. His finger slid in my ass and I knew it was over for me. I came all on his dick and he was right behind me. We were out of breath and wore out until I heard laughing. Looking over, Slim was standing there looking pissed.

SLIM...

These mufuckas got me fucked up. I was trying to take it easy on San because she was pregnant and here these bitches were fucking each other behind my back. I don't do disloyal shit and mufuckas was gone feel this one. Walking over to them, I sat down in my chair and just looked at them. Head had a nervous look on his face, because he already knew what was up.

"You two think you can cross me, in my office, and live to tell it? I'm thinking you dumber than you look. San, that was one hell of a risk you were willing to take."

"I'm sorry, I came here looking for you, but you weren't here. I thought it was cool because of the last time, if it's not, I'm sorry. It will never happen again."

"You damn right it's not. Get the fuck out of here and go home. If I catch you here and I didn't call you, imma kill your snake ass." She grabbed her shit and ran out of there fast as fuck. Head knew better, so he was sitting there looking stupid as fuck.

"Don't act like you're the only mufucka I'm supposed to fuck with. All I do is give you head most of the time, fuck out of here."

"Nigga do you not know she is part of a plan? I'm not fucking her just because. Only reason I let you in that day, is because I wanted some head. All of this shit is about Rogue. Not about no damn pussy. If all I wanted was the pussy, I would take care of my damn child. Rogue is about to die, and she is going to help us do it. Don't be out here fucking up the plan because you trying to get your dick wet."

"You should quit leaving me in the dark. If that was the plan, then you could have told me." Shaking my head, I wanted to slap his ass.

"Nigga, I don't have to tell you shit. Don't forget who the boss is. Rogue ass not gone see what hit him. He lucky I sent some rookies at his ass the last time. My next hitta won't miss. I saw a shadow coming our way and I stopped talking to see who it was.

"What up boss man. Trap number three finished earlier, I'm dropping the shit off. Since you here, you can put it up." Geno handed me three bags and I looked at him trying to read his mind. He looked like he always did, so I wasn't sure if he heard me or not. Making sure he kept his mouth closed, I decided to promote him.

"Come in here and sit down. I wanna holla at you about something. Head, give us a minute." When Head walked out, I continued to stare Geno in the eyes. He still carried his

RIGHT AND A WRONG WAY TO LOVE A DOPEBOY

nonchalant look he always did. That nigga didn't give a fuck about

shit but his money.

"What's good boss? You straight?"

"Yeah, I just been watching you and how you been getting

down. I think its time for you to get a promotion. You need to run

a crew because you have the potential to run it all. How you

handle your crew will be a test. How you take command will be a

test. Everything I throw at you, will be to see if you can do what

needs to be done, no matter what." I learned a long time ago,

that a nigga will sell his mama out for more money. If he heard

what I said, there was no way he would tell Rogue now.

"I got you. I'm always down to get more bread. You know

me a nigga got a football team around these parts."

"That's exactly what I wanted to hear. Your raise is

effective starting tomorrow. Let's get this money."

"Say less." Getting up, he dapped me up and walked out.

His first order of business would be to take out Head. If he did

that shit successfully, then I know he ready for the big time. Head liked to suck dick, but he was far from a bitch. His ass just chose the wrong one to cross. I don't know what he told that bitch, since they been creeping behind my back. What I did know was, that shit just got they ass a first way ticket to the dirt. You would think they would have chosen somewhere else to do it. When niggas get cocky, they get dead.

That's exactly what happened to Rogue. That nigga forgot who was in charge and I had to show him. I hate that his mama was the one that got hit. I wasn't that fucked up, but that was my fault sending them lil niggas to do the job. That was the reason they didn't speak up at the meeting. They didn't know what to say and was scared to put the wrong thing out there. If I hadn't spoken up, Rogue would have caught on.

These lil niggas ain't built the same. A mufucka like me would have been quick on my toes. All I need now is for San to get on board. I don't trust her to set him up, but I need her to let me know his every move. I can know exactly when to strike, if I knew where he was at all times. I just had to think of a good enough

178

reason for me to be following him. Bitches be thinking too much, and I didn't need her getting bigger than her thoughts. Yeah, I could black mail her, but the bitch might up and leave if she feels backed into a corner. I needed this to go smoothly, because Rogue was the strongest nigga on my roster. His ass didn't fear shit and wouldn't hesitate to take me out if he knew.

I wasn't going out like that and in my world it's either me or the next mufucka. Going home, I smiled at the way things were turning out. I wasn't the nigga in charge for shit. It was all about being the smartest nigga in the room, but I thought outside of the box. That bitch Raven skipped town, but I didn't need her at this point. I had something better. His homie Geno. When I got in the house, I sent him a text.

ME: You ready for your first job as a boss

G: You know it

ME: Take Head to meet his mama

G: How soon

ME: Yesterday my nigga

179

G: Say less

I would holla at San tomorrow. She was already feeling guilty and knew I was pissed. Hopefully I could use that to get her to do what I wanted. This plan had to be flawless. Head had to go first because he knew me too well. I couldn't allow him the room to think out a plan. His ass had to go.

To make sure the nigga was clueless, I think I will pay his mama a visit tomorrow. Take her some roses and shit to let her know how sorry I was, and we were out here looking for the niggas who did it. That shit would throw Rogue all the way off and I could use all the leverage I could get. Laughing at my genius, I pulled my phone out and tapped into my security at the warehouse. Going back to the video of San and Head tonight, I let it play as I pulled my dick out to jack off. Knowing he was about to be deader than Fred, I thought better of it and dialed his number. I may as well get one last hoorah in before his ass woke up dead.

RIGHT AND A WRONG WAY TO LOVE A DOPEBOY

I HATE U, I LOVE U

ROGUE...

Looking at San sleeping, I couldn't believe I was about to be a father. I never wanted this, well not with her anyway, but it was happening. Every time I tried to get excited about it, something in my gut kept giving me doubt. I know I'm the only nigga she been with, but I had a feeling she did some fuck shit to get pregnant. She wanted to win, and she was banking on me being a real nigga that wouldn't walk away from his child. That shit worked and now I was wondering if that was the right decision.

All the disappearing and secret calls or texts, had me side eyeing the shit out of her. I'm sure whatever it was, her friend Jen talked her into the shit. I hated that bitch and that was half the reason I always kept San at arm's length. She was easily influenced by that bitch and that shit pissed me off. We grown as fuck and you around here letting another bitch tell you what you should or shouldn't do. That was weak shit to me and that was a turn off. The more I stared at her, the more I realized her stomach should have been bigger. That means more than likely, she wasn't taking care of herself or some shit wasn't right. Sitting on the bed, I put my hand on her stomach and tried to feel for a kick or something. At eight months, I thought they be looking like whales. San looked good as shit and hadn't picked up that much weight. Her eyes opened, and she smiled at me.

"Why your stomach so small San?" The smile left, and she got aggravated.

"I don't know. Some people just carry well. Don't get mad at me because I look damn good pregnant. Bitches would kill to have my shape and I'm just glad I don't throw up and shit. The baby is fine and I'm fine. Quit worrying." Shit sounded good, but it sounded too good.

"I think I need to hear the doctors tell me you're good. If you're around here starving my baby, imma beat your ass. Even if you don't pick up weight, the baby should at least be getting bigger." She rolled her eyes and climbed out of bed. Opening her

robe, she stood in front of me.

"I don't even have stretch marks. It's okay, some people

just carry well. Ask anybody. You're stressing for nothing and you

gone have me worrying. Now, that shit ain't good for the baby."

"Aight, my bad. Can I get some pussy?"

"Baby, I told you my desire for that shit is gone. Blame it

on your child. I can't wait to drop this load, so I can get some

dick." That was another thing that threw me off, San has never

turned down sex, but she has been for months now. Trying to do

the right thing, I wasn't out here cheating, but the shit was

starting to get old.

"Yeah aight, but let me go try and fuck something, your ass

will be ready to fight."

"You damn right. I got some errands to run today, you

know grab some general shit for the baby. Can't do anything

major until the reveal." That was this new age shit. Mufuckas

didn't want to know what the sex was until they had a party or something. That was just an excuse to spend more money. I didn't care though, whatever she wanted was fine with me. Since she was going to be out baby shopping, I decided to stop by Lady house and ask her about the things San had just told me. When I pulled up, she was outside shoveling, and I couldn't have that. Getting out, I walked over to her and grabbed the shovel.

"Well ain't this nice. My son is over here doing some actual labor, not just bagging up drugs." I started to throw the snow at her ass, but I ducked that conversation.

"Next time, call me and tell me you need it done. I will have somebody come over here and clean this shit up. I came over here to talk, not freeze to death."

"If you quit trying to be cute and put on some clothes, you wouldn't be cold. Hurry up and finish, I'm going in to put on some cocoa for you." I laughed at how quick she got out of dodge. When I was done, I headed inside to talk to her. She was sitting at the table pouring us a cup. I loved when Lady babied me. Sometimes a nigga just wanted to be catered to. That made me miss Raven. She did everything for a nigga no questions asked and smiled while doing it.

"Lady, when a girl is eight months is it possible for her to be small? Is it a such thing as carrying a baby well or some shit?" She laughed and shook her head.

"Yes, it's a rare few women who will be small all the way to their birth. Some of them bitches don't get stretch marks, a big nose, or black necks. Us women who do get it, we say fuck them hoes. Why are you asking?" Shrugging my shoulders, I really don't know what was bugging me about it.

"Something just seems off to me. San is going on as if everything is fine, but it seems like she should be bigger or eating more. Slowing down and not on the go all the time. Hell, she's still wearing heels." Lady took it all in and sipped her cocoa.

"Tell her to come over for dinner. I got some stew in there and I will feel her out. A mama always knows son. We gone get to the bottom of it." Grabbing my phone, I shot her a text telling her my mama said come over. When she agreed, I got the strong urge

185

to talk to Raven. She had me blocked, but I just wanted to hear a voice that I knew didn't have an agenda with me.

"Lady let me see your phone." When she passed it to me, I dialed her number and hoped she answered. When I heard her voice, it was like time froze.

"Hello." I almost didn't say anything, but I knew she would hang up.

"Raven, it's Rogue. Don't hang up, I just want to talk to you. I needed to hear your voice."

"Boy fuck you." The phone hung up and I just stared at it. Lady shook her head at me and laughed.

"Call her back, tell her I want to talk to her. Maybe I can see how she is doing for you." Smiling, I knew there was no way Raven would turn her down. Lady was a genius. Dialing it back, I waited for her to pick up again.

"Quit calling my fucking phone."

"Raven, Lady wants to talk to you. Don't hang up."

186

"Boy, fuck her too." When the phone hung up, I was shocked. She loved the shit out of my mama, so I knew I had hurt her beyond repair. When I dialed it back, she had the number blocked.

"Well damn. You done hurt her so bad, she don't fuck with the bitch that made ya. Savage. I think your bitch at the door." That was weird because I thought she was going to the mall. Getting up, I let her in and she said she changed her mind and sat down.

"Hey Lady, how you doing?" My mama stared at her. She smiled, but I could tell she was reading her.

"What's up San. You looking good girl. I wish I had carried that well. When is my grandbaby due?" It took her a second, then she answered.

"Thank you and in a month. I can't wait. We're having a gender reveal in a couple of weeks, you coming?"

"You already know I'll be there. It's some stew in there if you want some. You know you have to keep that baby fed. I need

187

me a chunky grandbaby." They both laughed, and I couldn't tell if something was off or not. Lady never stopped laughing and smiling. They talked for about thirty more minutes and I was dying to know what Lady thought.

"San, you think you can fix your man a plate. I'm hungry than a mufucka and y'all trying to talk all night and shit. I don't know shit about an epidolo. I'm hungry shit." They both fell the fuck out and she stood up to go get me a plate. As soon as she was through the doors, Lady turned to me and her smile faded.

"Something ain't right with her or that pregnancy. Usually if you ask a mother to be when their due date is, they give you an actual date. She doesn't know and that doesn't make sense. Yeah, she is carrying well, but her stomach is not big enough. It doesn't have to be huge, but it's off to me. Be careful son. A woman scorned will do anything."

"See that's what I'm saying. It's not nothing there specifically out of order, but it just feels off. Everything she said from the beginning, she's still saying. It just gives me the wrong

RIGHT AND A WRONG WAY TO LOVE A DOPEBOY

feeling whenever we talk about the baby. You start asking too many questions, she always find a way to change the subject. Maybe she just doesn't give a fuck about the baby and all she cares about is that it got her to win."

"That could be son. Whatever it is, you need to figure it out. I can't do it for you, I have some other shit on my plate I need to handle."

"What do you have to handle?" Shrugging her shoulders, she smiled at me.

"My business son. That's my business." San came walking out of the back with my food and I slammed that shit. San ass could cook, she just didn't do it often no more. Always talking about the baby got her tired. Seems the baby don't want her to do shit no more. Looking at the time, I got up and kissed Lady on the jaw, then San.

"I gotta go pick up some money. I'll be home in a lil while San. You don't have to leave, you can spend some time with Lady. You know she old and be lonely as hell." Lady picked up a roll and

189

threw it at me. Shit hit me dead in the forehead and they both fell the fuck out laughing. "You falling off Lady. Your bread didn't used to be so hard." Before she could respond, I walked out the door and made my runs. When I got to the warehouse to count it, Geno was in there doing the same. He never counted the money, so this was odd to me.

"What up Rogue nigga. Hurry up and count your money, so we can go have a drink or something. I ain't kicked it with you in a minute." Nodding my head, I sat down and handled my business.

RAVEN...

I was in the house pacing back and forth, while I talked to myself. All this time I hadn't heard from him, now the day before my baby shower, his bitch ass called. He had me fucked up, him and his bald headed ass mama. Lady should have swallowed his ass, since she didn't, I hated her bitch ass too. Gone call back and say Lady wants to talk to you like that was gone make me bend. That only tells me, he thinks he still has a hold on me. Nigga can hold deez nuts by the hair underneath. All I wanted to do was forget this nigga existed. I had enough shit on my plate and I wasn't for all the bullshit.

I don't know what it's like to be a mother. The only guidelines I had to go by, was what my mama showed me. That was a disaster waiting to happen and I was starting to get scared. I don't want to be a bad mom, I needed to break the cycle, but I wasn't sure I knew how. Everyone else had more faith in me, than I had in myself. I could feel myself starting to panic and the baby kicked. She didn't like when I got worked up and that always scared me. She could feel when I was pissed off.

"Why the fuck are you in here talking to yourself? You starting to lose it. You ready for your big day tomorrow?" Coi always popped up at the craziest times. It's like she could feel when my mind was shifting.

"That nigga called me and then tried to use his rusty ass mama as an excuse for me to stay on the phone. I'm just trying to move on with my life and his ass can't be pulling these stunts in order for me to do that." She had a disappointing look on her face and I knew her ass was about to talk shit.

"Sis, don't you think it's unfair for you to make him miss all of this. I'm sure he would want to be a part of the baby shower. If he ever finds out, that shit not gone go well." Rolling my eyes as hard as I could, I wobbled over to the bed and climbed in.

"Fuck him. I don't care what he would like to be a part of. Hell, I would have loved to have been a part of his life. He chose the family he wanted to be with and I'm okay with that. I suggest you do the same."

"Bitch you tried it. He chose that family because he didn't know he had another one. Hell, replaying the shit in my mind, I don't remember him choosing her. You basically said it for him and left." Sitting up, I tried to calm myself. She was about to piss me off.

"He didn't correct me or try to stop me. Nigga not once called or even tried to come find me. His ass made that decision and now he has to live with it. Last I checked, this was my life, my child, and my body. I don't need permission to do shit and I damn

sure ain't asking for suggestions."

"Who the fuck you think you talking to Raven? Don't play

me like I'm some bitch off the streets. I'm the one wiping your

tears every fucking night. I'm the one that's been handling shit for

the baby's arrival. I don't see your ass in there painting or putting

cribs together. I've been to every fucking doctor's appointment

and I don't give a fuck what you don't want to hear. Fuck around

and play yourself."

"Bitch fuck you too. I don't need you, like I don't need him.

You think you done did some shit because you're there holding

the tissue. Bitch I'm the one going through the pain, the

pregnancy, and all the bullshit to go along with it. Just because

you sat your big nose ass there and held the bucket, does not give

you the right to tell me what the fuck I should do. You can let

yourself the fuck out of my house."

"Oh bitch, you better be lucky you pregnant or I would

drag your ass all over this mufucka. Don't write a check your ass can't cash bitch. If I walk away, your orphan ass got nothing.

Cheryl is my mama bitch, yours is dead." She turned to walk away,

and my mouth hit the floor. I can't believe she said that to me.

That shit hurt me bad, but I knew I had said some fucked up shit

as well. Crazy part is, I didn't even mean it. By the time it left my

mouth, it was too late to take it back. Coi and my aunt have been

everything to me, but she just showed me that they could leave in

the drop of a dime as well. Wiping my face, I cried myself to sleep.

****

Looking in the mirror, I was over how I looked. It was my

baby shower and I looked a mess. I cried all night and I knew

nobody was going to be here. All I had was Coi and my aunt, that's

why I told them I didn't need a baby shower, but they insisted. I

could feel the tears about to fall again and I was over it. My ass

was about to climb back in bed.

"Awwww you look so pretty. I never thought I would see

the day my other daughter would give me a grandbaby. Hurry

your ass up, I'm sure the guests are waiting on you." My aunt

194

Cheryl was beaming with pride and I was sure she hadn't talked to Coi, until she walked in the room

"Come on lil ugly, let me do your make up. I knew your sissy ass was up here crying and I can't have you looking fucked up." Smiling, I walked over to her and hugged her the best way I could with my big ass belly. We both were sorry and knew we were wrong, so no words needed to be said.

"You sure all this hair looks right on me? I want to cut this or something. I'm hot and I haven't even walked down the stairs yet." This was my first sew in and I didn't know what to do with all this hair.

"You look perfect baby mama. Now quit frowning, so I can get your make up just right. You need to be cute for your pictures." I knew Coi like that back of my hand and this bitch was up to something. When she was done we walked downstairs and jumped in my Audi sports car. Me and Coi was looking like twins in our black button ups and slacks, pink bow tie with suspenders, and pink heels. My feet was probably busting out of my shoes

195

though because these dogs were barking, but we looked cute. We arrived at the hall and I got out expecting it to be empty as hell, but I was shocked to see all of my readers there. Taj, Sierra, Nesha, Marla, Tannesia, Misha, Charlotte, Donique, Kira, Kisa. Oh my God, it was so many there, I didn't know what to do.

Tiff, Chey, Chels, Doodles, Victoria. Joan, Mandy, Erica, Jasmine, Lavora, Shawna. Regina, Lani, Huanna, Shontea. It was so many people. I prayed no one got upset because I forgot their names, but it was so many I couldn't stop crying. They all hugged me and showed me so much love, I can't believe I ever felt alone. No matter what I went through in my life, my career, or my own fucked up space, my readers were there for me. They were like distant family that was always rooting for me even when I wanted to give up on myself. They believed in me, even when I thought I wasn't good enough.

Coi smiled at me and knew the emotions I was going through, and I couldn't stop smiling, until I saw her. She was in the corner looking nervous and I was ready to slap her and Coi bitch ass to sleep. She had invited Lady. When I saw her coming towards me, I wanted to run, but my feet wouldn't allow me to move. A bitch was stuck, and I prayed he wasn't here. She reached out her arms to hug me, but I kept mine down by my side.

"Hey baby girl. Why didn't you tell us? You know we would have been here for you. There is no way he would have let you go through this by yourself. I'm so sorry for everything." In my mind, I was screaming fuck you get out.

"I didn't tell you, because I didn't want you to know. You came all this way, so you can stay. Let's be clear though, if you tell your son, I won't ever allow you all to see her or be a part of her life."

"Raven…"

"Do I have your word?"

"Yes." She said that shit reluctantly, but I didn't give a fuck. This was going to be done on my terms and no one was going to force me to do it their way.

197

"I don't want him to ever be around my child or to know about her. If you would like the privilege of being there, I won't stop that. You did nothing to deserve this, but if you tell him, I'll move and neither of you will see her. He made his choice and she is mine. Not Rogue's." Lady looked hurt, but I could tell she didn't want to miss out on seeing her.

"I'm so sorry for how he hurt you. I've never lied to my son, but I will not go against your wishes. I hope that one day, you will change your mind. He talks about you all the time and I have to watch the hurt on his face every time he says your name."

"With all due respect Lady, I really don't give a fuck." Walking off, I went to go mingle with the rest of the guests. It hurt me to treat her that way, but I was so angry, I was taking the shit out on everybody. I gave Coi a look letting her know she went too far. Not allowing it to ruin my day, I put on a fake smile and smiled for the cameras.

GOSSIP

SLIM...

I was starting to think Geno wasn't the right person for the job. His ass was avoiding me I think. Whenever I came to the warehouse, the nigga be done already come and gone. His ass handled all the business I needed him to handle, but I still needed this other shit done. Even though he didn't tell Rogue what I planned to do, that nigga was loyal and stayed out of business he felt had nothing to do with him.

It was time I gave him a different perspective. See, I could take Rogue and Geno out myself, but if shit went wrong, mufuckas would look at me like I was flaw. Geno could take the fall and I would take him out if shit went bad. Everyone pretty much knew what times I came by the warehouse, so on today, I came earlier. When I saw Geno's car outside, I put my plan in motion. The fact that Rogue wasn't here was perfect. Making sure my phone was on silent, I pretended to be on the phone when I walked inside. Motioning for Geno to come to my office, I

continued to have a fake conversation. Closing my door, I went

behind my desk acting as if I was stressed the fuck out.

"Look, none of that shit got anything to do with my

money. He brings in more than any other worker and he been on

the team for a minute. Shorty got this, and I need y'all to

understand I know what I'm doing." I got silent as if the fake

person on the phone was giving their point of view on the matter.

"I really don't give a fuck what you and Head agree on.

This is my shit and I know what the fuck I'm doing. Low key, I think

y'all hating on Geno and that ain't how we do business. As long as

he does his job, his ass gone keep climbing the ladder." Geno was

paying attention now, and I know he wanted to hear who was on

the other end of the phone.

"Rogue I never said your spot was in question. Y'all can run

this shit together though. It's enough bread for everybody out

here to eat my nigga." Truth was, Rogue came to me the other

day telling me once he found out who hit his mama, he was

walking away. We got into it hard and he didn't give a fuck what I had to say. The nigga had no respect and I was tired of playing with his bitch ass. This wasn't no movie shit, nigga don't get to decide he wants to just up and leave the game. It's levels to this shit. His ass was on his way out, but not the way he thought.

"We'll talk about this later, but ain't shit gone change. The lil nigga earned his spot and y'all niggas just gotta accept that. Head is cancelled any fucking way. Nigga stealing and he talking about taking a member of the crew out, that shit unacceptable. I'll get at you." Hanging up, I tried to read his face, but as usual, you couldn't tell what that nigga was thinking.

"What up boss man?" That was all he said just like usual.

"Look, this shit getting out of hand and I'm tired of playing peace maker. I'm sorry you had to hear that shit, but maybe it was good that you did. These niggas don't like the fact that you moving up the ladder and they getting flaky. As a boss, you have to know when to eliminate a problem before it gets bad."

"I hear all that, but what does any of this gotta do with me. They mad, but they don't have a choice but to accept it." His ass never wanted to be in other people beef.

"Let me show you something." Typing in the date and time I wanted, I pulled up the video of Head and San fucking in the office. Turning the camera around, I let him watch what was on the screen. "This nigga done violated in the worse way. Not only is he sleeping with Rogue's girl, he talking about taking you out. He doesn't know I'm aware of any of this shit and he gotta go." He nodded, and I knew I had him.

"Shorty a freak. Hey, I'm all for it, just say when and I got you. Niggas can't be doing fowl ass shit like this and walk the streets after." I smiled on the inside.

"Right now. I don't know when he calls his self coming at you, and I refuse to give him opportunity."

"Say less." Standing up, we left out and jumped in my whip. I pulled my phone out and texted Head letting him know I was on the way be naked for me. I knew saying that would give him the impression that I was going to fuck him. His ass was too thirsty not to do what I asked. As soon as I pulled up, I told Geno how to get in and what room was his. Not asking any questions, he got out and headed inside. Five minutes later, he was walking back to the car as if nothing happened. When he climbed in, I thought the nigga bitched up.

"Did you do it? What happened?" His ass tossed a severed dick at me and I screamed like a bitch.

"Didn't I say I was gone do it? The nigga was up there naked and never saw it coming. Figured you wanted proof and I wasn't about to take all day with this lil ass knife bringing you a head." I laughed and pulled off. This lil nigga was crazy as hell and I knew I picked the right person.

"You know we gone have to take the homie out next though right?" He looked at me as if he didn't know who I was referring to. "Rogue, he's not gone want you to be his boss. If you not ready to go to war with him, you gone have to do him before he does you."

203

"I know. It's all good. He's a lot harder than Head. I'll have to study that nigga and figure out where he goes. I got you, no doubt boss." This nigga deserved a dumb ass bonus.

"Imma give you a bonus behind this shit. When it's all over, you'll be right hand. Don't worry about finding out his routes and shit. I'll get that. You just make sure you don't miss. The last niggas fucked up and hit his mama." Geno looked at me and smirked.

"Nigga I don't miss. Right hand sounding good as fuck right about now. Get me the routes and I got you. The walls be listening sometimes, so don't call me at the warehouse. Only hit me from your crib where you know it's safe. This nigga is a beast, we have to be careful as hell taking him out."

"I got you. Congrats lil nigga. You done made it to the top." If the lil nigga gave head, he would be perfect. I knew better than to ask some shit like that though, so I dropped him off. I knew where I had to go to get my fix and it was time to put this bitch to work. I was gone miss the fuck out of Head, but he had out served his purpose. On top of that, he betrayed me. Nobody fucks

something that belongs to me. Grabbing my phone, I called

Rogue.

"What up Slim?"

"I need you to swing by the warehouse and hold it down

for me until I get back. I won't be gone long, but I need someone

there since we don't know who after us. I would rather it be you,

them lil niggas can't hold the fort down."

"Say less." Hanging up, I drove towards his house. Yeah, I

was a bold nigga.

SAN...

"Hey, I know that I don't want to know what I'm having

until the reveal, but that don't mean you can't know." Handing

Rogue the envelope the doctors gave me, I smiled. I finally got the

sex of the baby and now I could plan the damn reveal for real. My

ass was out here faking errands and shit just so he didn't get

suspicious. The closer it got, I swear the harder this shit was to lie about it. He put the envelope in his pocket and smiled at me.

Kissing me on my jaw, he grabbed his keys.

"I'll look when I get away from your nosey ass. I know you gone want to see if I open it in front of you and react. The minute I get excited, your ass gone be all over my back. Get you some rest, I'll be back as soon as I can."

"Okay, don't stay gone too long. The baby gets riled up when you're not around. I guess that means they miss you." He smiled, and I swear for some reason, I knew everything was going to be okay. When he walked out of the door, my phone rang and seeing it was Jen, I answered.

"Go best friend that's my best friend. Ohhhhh you betta. Who is your mother fucking best friend bitch?" I laughed because she was being extra as fuck.

"Is there a reason you screaming in my ear doing the most right now? Your ass always lit and shit." We laughed, but she was still excited.

"You still ain't answer the question."

206

"You're my best friend, now please tell me why you're so excited." This bitch gave a dramatic ass pause and I was ready to hang up on her ass.

"So, you know Ke Ke is a CNA at Rush hospital and she told me she fucking this doctor. I told her about my friend that needed to close the time gap on her pregnancy and she said, you take castor oil and it makes you go in labor early. Her man will deliver the baby and you can pay him to say the baby has some type of complications or something instead of it being premature."

"Wait what?"

"Look bitch, I may be explaining it kind of mixed up, but I think that's right. I got her number for you, but basically, you're in the clear as long as you pay that bread. You just need to call her and find out how much."

"Will my baby be okay being born that early?"

"Yes, the doctor said the baby will be fine." I would only be six months and I didn't think it automatically put the baby in the clear, but I was willing to do it if it meant keeping Rogue. I would just pray extra hard that my baby was a fighter like me. I didn't want anything to happen to my baby.

"Okay, set it up. I'll do it." My text went off and I saw it was Slim.

S: Open the front door

"San, did you hear me?"

"Let me call you back." Hanging up, I walked down the stairs slowly. I know damn well this nigga wasn't at Rogue's house. It's as if he was trying to get me caught up. When I opened the door, sure enough, his ass was standing right there.

"Are you going to invite me in?" My body was shaking I was so damn scared. Moving out the way, I allowed him to walk in.

"What are you doing here? You know he can come back at any moment?"

"He'll be gone until I get back. San, I need you to do me a favor. These meetings are getting harder to do and I'm almost at the point where I want to say fuck it and just tell Rogue. Shit ain't

208

worth the hassle or worth me getting caught. If you would rather keep doing this instead of me telling him, I need to know where this nigga at when he leaves the house. I'm the one taking all the risks and need to know that I can trust you."

"You do know he doesn't tell me his every move. I have been taking the risks as well and I'm the one that can lose everything." His ass smirked.

"Then you need to do better about finding out where your man is actually going. I'm not about to get caught slipping and die over some pussy." This nigga act like he had to have my coochie.

"Or we could just stop fucking."

"You carrying my baby. I don't want another nigga fucking you while you got my child in you. That is the reason Head is no longer with us." I knew that nigga was threatening me, and I was tired of it. I loved fucking Head, but I liked fucking him as well. All the extra shit wasn't needed.

"Okay, I'll try to keep up with him more. I'll shoot you a text when I know something. Now you have to leave before he

209

catches us in his house. That nigga will kill us dead if he came home and found you here."

"I told you, he's gone until I get back. Let me worry about where he is today. You pick up after that. Right now, I just need you to come over here and suck my dick. We'll be fucking a lot more now. My girl left me and imma need to get some release." I prayed he was right about Rogue not coming home. Walking over to him, I grabbed his pants and went to pull them down. "Not right here. I want you in his bed." Slowly walking upstairs, I said a silent prayer before we went in the room. By the time I got on the bed, his dick was out and pointing at my lips.

Taking him in, I started sucking that shit like I loved it. My ass was horny as hell and I may as well enjoy it since I had to do it. I hadn't been fucking Rogue or Head since Slim caught us. This pussy was aching. Making sure my mouth was wet as hell, I gave him some sloppy wet neck work. His ass was going crazy and his knees was buckling. Pushing me away, he nodded for me to get on the bed. Doing as he asked, he walked over to me and flipped me over. His dick was inside of me before I could get on my knees good. For some reason, that dick was putting in work tonight. As if he had a point to prove. His ass was going to work, and I couldn't stop the moans or the screams from escaping my lips. Snatching his dick out of me, he aimed at the pillow and came all over it. That nigga was beyond petty and I was over irritated with his bitch ass for that move.

"I'll be calling you. Make sure you do as we talked about." He grabbed his phone and sent a text. Walking in the bathroom, he washed his dick off and then left out. Jumping up, I sprayed the room and started pulling the sheets and stuff off the bed. As soon as I got them in the washer, Rogue walked in. When he got upstairs, he looked at the bed and at me.

"I threw up everywhere. I'm putting some new ones on now." He nodded, but I wasn't sure if he believed me. This shit was getting messy and I needed a way out.

MONA LISA

ROGUE...

In my line of work, I tend to let unnecessary shit slide. You had to choose which battles were important and which ones weren't. Sometimes, your anger could have you reacting and doing some shit that end up getting you caught up. You could never move based off emotion. You had to think of everything as business. If it wasn't helping you out in a money sense, then there was no need for the war. Of course, sometimes, shit didn't work out like that. Sometimes, you had to fuck a nigga up to show them who the fuck you are. In this case, that's exactly what it was.

See, Slim had crossed the line and that nigga had to pay. His order caused my mama to get shot and he has no idea I knew it. Slim was the boss, but I was the mufucka that they respected. I made sure everybody in the streets ate. I've been silent, but I never stopped looking for the nigga that shot Lady. I could never

212

let that fly, especially after she gave me the okay. Lady never agreed with anything I did in the streets, so that meant something to me. Not knowing who I could trust in the crew, I was gone need San to help me out. I'm not sure if she would agree, but I was going to explain how important this shit was. She was so happy lately, and I just watched her dancing as she cleaned up the house. When she saw me watching her, she walked over to me and smiled.

"Why you looking at me like that?" Pulling her down next to me, I stared her in the eyes.

"Because you're beautiful as fuck. Sometimes I forget just how sexy you are, even with the baby. Your looks can save our family." Now, she looked confused. "You have always been my rider and I need you to do this one last thing. Once it's over, I'm out the game for good. I already told Slim I was done, so there is nothing left to do after this." You could see the excitement in her eyes.

"What do you need from me baby?"

213

"I need you to fuck Slim." She almost choked on her own spit and I damn near had to do CPR on her ass.

"Have you lost your fucking mind? There is no way I'm doing that shit, you got me fucked up. The fact that you would even ask me that shows me you don't give a fuck about me." The tears fell, and I rubbed my finger down her face to wipe them away.

"San look. I know that's some fucked up shit to ask you, but a woman is every nigga's downfall. You won't have to fuck him more than once. I just need you to get him drunk, fuck him, and keep him up there long enough for me to clean his safe out. By the time he realizes what happened, we'll be long gone."

"Baby, I don't want to. What if something goes wrong? I don't want to fuck another nigga." I was getting frustrated, so I pushed her buttons.

"I fucked Raven and I know you never got over that, but you forgave me. You're not cheating, I'm asking you to fuck this nigga, so I can get out the game and we can leave like you always wanted. Hell, I could buy you an island if you do this one thing for me. I got you, I just need you to have my back." She cried, but she nodded her head ok.

"I'll do it, but please don't get us killed."

"Aight, imma stay here. Go to the warehouse now, that nigga there. Getting up, I went to the closet and got a bottle of White Hennessy and gave it to her. "Have him get drunk, he will take you home. Text me when you get there, and you know what to do after that. Leave like normal and we're on the first plane out this bitch."

"Okay." She was shaking when she left out and I hope she didn't fuck this shit up. Grabbing my keys, I headed to Slim's house. I wasn't going to wait for them to get there, I would already be waiting on them. I would be able to get all the nigga's money with no problem. Waiting on the porch, I hid until I heard his car go in the garage. I knew his alarm was disabled, so I jimmied the lock on the front door and went in. Staying in the shadows, I watched as he stumbled trying to get upstairs. He was kissing San grabbing her ass, all while trying to stand up. He was fucked up and I had to fight my laugh. He finally got upstairs, and I followed them. I stood outside the door listening to him talk shit saying how he was about to tear her pussy up. My phone went off and I got the text from San.

"Ride my face." Seconds later, you could hear San screaming and I could tell she wasn't faking. I knew when she was turned on to the max and she was in heaven right now. Shaking my head, I kept my cool and stood there. Slapping noises started coming from the room, so I knew they was fucking. You could hear how juicy her pussy was and I knew she wasn't upset about having to fuck this nigga.

Hearing the door close downstairs, I waited and gave them a couple more minutes before I walked in. Pulling the burner gun I had, I walked in the room. Both of their eyes were closed and they was screaming and moaning as she rode him. When I put the gun to her lips, she opened her eyes. I had my finger to my lips and she did as she was told. I'm sure she didn't think I would be here

216

that fast. Grabbing her hands, I made her put them around the

gun and point it at Slim. His ass was shaking, so I knew he had just

cum.

"Hey nigga surprise." His eyes opened, and he looked at

me in disbelief.

"I promise she came on to me. I'm drunk and fucked up,

I'm sorry nigga, but let's not lose no money behind a hoe." I

laughed at his clown ass.

"I know she came on to you, I sent her bitch." Geno

walked in making sure that Slim saw him before I forced San to

pull the trigger. She screamed like crazy and jumped off his dick.

Grabbing a sheet, she tried to wipe the blood off.

"Why the fuck would you do that? You said rob him not kill

him."

"I know, but I needed to know I could trust you. If you ever

walked away or vice versa, you could never tell. You were the one

that pulled the trigger. This gun will be put up as an insurance

policy. You will never open your mouth, or you will spend the rest

217

of your life in jail. Now get dressed, we got a lot of money to get out of the floor in the basement. Geno, once we split this money up, the streets are yours. You deserve it my nigga. Once they find his body, I'll make an official announcement to the crew."

"Good looking my nigga." Slim didn't realize Geno would always be loyal to me. I met that nigga when he was homeless. I like the way he tried to work for some food rather than ask for a hand out. I bought him and his family a house. It hurt my heart to see a nigga trying to provide for his family but couldn't.

I stocked their house with food, furniture, and bought them clothes. The next day, I took him to Slim and got him put on. There was nothing a mufucka could tell him about me. That nigga was like blood to me. We went downstairs and took everything. I don't know where he kept the rest of his money, but we got a million apiece and that was enough. Making sure we wiped San's prints off everything, we got the fuck up out of there and loaded the car.

"I'll see you at the gender reveal shit tomorrow."

218

"Say less boss." We laughed and went our separate ways. You could tell San was still a little shook up, but it was over now.

****

I knew what was inside the envelope, so I didn't wear pink or blue. I put on all white and headed downstairs. San was already waiting on me in her pink. Leaving out, we got in the car and headed to the banquet hall for this dumb ass party. When we pulled up, I could see Lady was already there and so was Geno. I rapped with them for a minute and then we all went inside. Lady had on Blue, but Geno was neutral like me.

Everyone was walking around in their colors happy as hell and I had never seen San smile so much. Her and Jen was over there falling out and I knew they ass was up to no good. Walking up to the front of the room, I grabbed the mic. Everyone looked at me smiling ready to see what the doting father had to say.

"Can I have everyone's attention please. I know San has this big reveal coming at the end, but I just wanted to thank you all for coming. Only two of my people are here with me, but the

219

outpouring of love from San's side is amazing. I have a video slide

prepared for you, to show you how much San loves me."

Everyone laughed, and San looked at me with so much love on her

face. Pushing play, the videos started going. Everyone's smile

started to slowly fade, when they realized it was San fucking a

nigga that wasn't me. It also showed, her riding a nigga's face

while he got his dick sucked.

"What the fuck is this Rogue? Are you fucking kidding

me?" I laughed and made sure my gun was visible just in case one

of them was feeling froggy.

"No I'm not, but you had to be when you tried to pass a

fag's baby off as mine. You fucked these booty bandits damn near

every day and came home to me like it was nothing. I knew it was

weird that your stomach wasn't getting big. I visited your doctor

dummy and your ass is only five months. No, they weren't

supposed to give me your records, but mufuckas will do anything

when a guns to their head. You all enjoy your reveal for a baby

that is nowhere ready to come out yet. Oh, by the way, it's a boy.

You got a little booty bandit on the way. Y'all be easy now." With that, I dropped the mic leaving her screaming my name. We walked out, and Lady started going off.

"Nigga you could have told me what you were doing. I would have worn my project hair and tennis shoes. You got me out here looking like the bell of the ball and hoes ready to fight us. You know I'm bald head, so I have to be prepared for fights and shit. Bring your dumb ass on before the big bitch come out here and grab me." Laughing we jumped in our cars and pulled off.

RAVEN...

Walking around my house, I continued to watch the clock waiting to see if the contractions would get closer. Them bitches was hitting me hard, but they weren't close enough together yet. The hospital will fuck around and tell me it's Braxton Hicks or something like that and I wasn't going. When I walked in that bitch, I wanted to be sure my ass was in labor.

Ahhhhh... I don't see how anyone did this shit more than once. The way this pain was hitting me, I never wanted to do this again. It's fucked up I had to do this alone, but I refused to give in and let Rogue be here. Fuck him. I did tell Lady when they first started though. My ass was talking shit while I was pacing and hit a slippery patch and damn near went down in a split. My damn water had broken, and it was time for me to get the fuck out of here. Not ready to hit the floor, I grabbed my bag and got ready to leave. When I opened the door, Coi was right there.

"I felt it in my spirit your vagina was stretching baby mama. Bring your ass and you better not have this baby in my car." Laughing, I waddled towards her until another contraction hit me. Reaching out, I couldn't grab shit but her titty, so I squeezed that mufucka until it passed. "Oh hell no, you got me fucked up. Get your ass in the back seat." We got in the car and that hoe literally put me in the back like I was the fucking help.

She took off to the hospital and if she didn't swing the baby out of me, I damn sure would have whip lash from all the quick turns she was doing. When we got to the door, a bitch was happy as shit. I jumped out of the car and damn near ran inside.

"Ma'am can we help you?"

"I'm in labor. Well I think I'm still in labor, you might want to check her back seat for the baby. She may have swerved her right on out." Everybody laughed, but I was dead ass. They took me up to labor and delivery and I needed some drugs.

"Sis don't get the drugs, you can do this natural. It will be over before you know it."

"Bitch, it feels like my ass is hanging out. I need drugs, please just give me a little." She seemed to find the shit funny as hell, but I was in so much pain I was delirious. Lady walked in and I tried to play on her feelings.

"Please Lady, I need a hit. Just one, tell them to give me some drugs. This shit hurts and I can't take it. Please."

"It will be over soon baby girl. Trust me, do something to take your mind off it." That bitch wasn't helping, and I don't even know why I called her. She can take her old ass back home.

223

"You can read your comments on FB. I posted from your phone that you were in labor as if I was you. Bitch your page blowing up."

"Really bitch. Lady, put her out and bring me some drugs. You're my only friend. Everyone else hates me." This old bald headed huzzy wasn't paying me any attention. She was typing on her phone and ignoring the shit out of me. "WHY ARE YALL HERE IF YOU'RE NOT GOING TO HELP ME?" Lady looked up and laughed with Coi. This baby wasn't coming fast enough, and I knew I should have made that nigga wear a condom.

Three hours later, I looked like a rundown prostitute that was fucking in one hundred degree weather in a car with no air, and the windows were up. My mouth was dry, and my hair was stuck to my face from all the sweat. How the fuck was my head getting moisture but not my mouth.

"Bitch when you gone push? You in here looking like side show Bob." I couldn't even laugh I was in so much pain. These mufuckas was getting a good laugh at my expense and I was sick of it. All they were feeding me was ice chips and that shit wasn't helping.

"Mommy, let me check you again." I wanted to kick the bitch in her chin, but I let her see if the baby was ready. When she smiled at me, I wanted to sigh out of relief. "She's ready."

"Thank God. Bitch quit smiling and come on." They all laughed as she propped my legs up to push. I thought I was ready until I went to push the first time. That felt worse than the contractions.

"Come on mommy, I need you to push." I was crying, and the shit hurt so bad.

"I can't. I'm sorry. Please, it hurt so bad."

"Yes you can. Come on Shorty, you got this." Looking over at the door, Rogue was standing there looking sexy as fuck. Even though his ass looked suckable right now, I did not want him here.

"Coi, when this baby gets out of me, I'm beating your mother fucking ass. I DON'T WANT HIS BIG LIP ASS HERE."

"She didn't tell me. I checked your Facebook and saw that you posted you was in labor. I found it funny since I didn't know you was pregnant. Right now, none of that matters. I need you to push before you hurt the baby. Come on, push I got you." He walked over and grabbed my hand. Tired of fighting, I didn't pull away. Leaning my head against his stomach, I cried as I pushed.

Baby Dalia was born, and I couldn't stop looking at her. She was perfect. I had been ignoring the fact that Rogue was in the room after the baby was born. He stayed quiet and out of the way. I guess he thought, I would put him out. Looking over to him, I passed him the baby, so that he could see her. He began to cry and no matter how mad I was at him or what would happen in the future, this moment was perfect.

"Thank you for letting me stay. I missed so much baby girl, but I'm here now. I will never leave your side. I'm here now baby, daddy's here." He was crying, and I couldn't figure out why. Nigga was acting like it was his first child. Fake ass bitch. Even though it was a beautiful sight to see, he didn't need to stand his ass in here like he was a first time father. Lady was crying and taking pictures as well. Not wanting to ruin their moment, I just watched them. I heard chuckling and I looked over at Coi. She found this shit real funny and I didn't.

I wanted his ass gone and my baby to myself. I only agreed to give Lady a piece of her life. I wasn't prepared to share her completely. Rogue was going to want her around all the time, but that shit wasn't happening. I won't take away his happiness now, but the minute he gets to talking about visitation, I was going to snatch that rug right from under his ass.

"Can I get a pic of all of you please?" Lady was on some we are family type shit and I wanted to tell her ass fuck off. Instead, I nodded and smiled as he came and stood next to me with the baby. I hope my hair was matted and I had a booger in my nose.

YOUR CHILD

ROGUE...

Me and Lady was in the waiting room and I was two seconds away from beating her ass. She knew that Raven was pregnant and didn't tell me. I was so hurt and angry, all I could do was mean mug her ass. She knew how I felt about her. Hell, she even knew what I went through with San, but her ass still chose to keep her mouth closed. When she went out of town last month, I thought that shit sounded fishy. I thought she had found a man on the low, but her ass had come out here to the baby shower.

"How do you not tell your child something like this? I would never keep something from you if I thought it would hurt you. I missed out on so much, why would you do this to me."

"Look nigga, it was either me or you. She said if I told you, she would move and neither of us would be able to see the baby. At least someone from your side was able to be in the baby's life. Don't get mad at me because you chose the wrong hoe. Plus you ain't miss shit, I got a lot of pictures." This mufucka was laughing and thought the shit was funny.

"Ma, this is my child, my life. The shit is not funny. I don't see how you could sit over there and laugh like it is." Shrugging her shoulders, she sat down in the chair.

"It would be funny to you as well if you weren't over there acting light skinned. Besides, it's the truth. One of us should have been here, she didn't want you around. When she asked me to come, I made sure I brought my camera, so you didn't miss a thing. I'm sorry if that hurt you El Debarge, but it's about the baby." I could understand that, but the shit still was fucked up. I'm her child and even if she said, you can't come, but I'm telling you because you deserve to know, I would have been okay with that. I would have tried to fix my mess without Raven knowing she told me.

"I get why you did it ma, but it was another way to do that, so that your child didn't end hurt. It's so much anger inside of me, but I'm happy at the same time."

229

"Let that hurt go sus. Your baby girl is here and healthy. My chunky baby pretty as hell and you were there to witness her birth. You talking shit, but I didn't have to text you and tell you she had a Facebook page. You witnessed it and that's all that matters."

"Now I'm sis because you over there looking like Deacon Fry. Patchy head ass."

"I didn't have time to find my good wig. She called me, and I ran out the door. I didn't want to miss my flight." We both laughed, but I started to get nervous. I didn't know how this birth shit went, so I wasn't sure if the baby could get sick two days later. The doctor had been in there with them for two hours. Coi told me she would come get us as soon as they were done. The longer it took, the more I started to panic. Not being able to take much more of this, I got up and went to the desk. If something was wrong, I needed them to tell me what it was. I prayed I didn't get any more bad news, because I really didn't think I could take it. The nurse looked at me like I was crazy.

"Excuse me, can you tell me if Raven Woods and baby girl Wright are doing okay? We've been waiting a long time for the doctor to come out of the room."

"I'm sorry, but they were discharged a couple of hours ago. I'm sorry, but they are gone." I looked at her like she was crazy and made her check twice before I went back over to Lady.

"Son are they okay? What's wrong?"

"That bitch was discharged and left. She didn't want us to know and they snuck off. I have no idea where Raven went with my daughter. Grabbing my phone, I called her, and my number was blocked. "Lady, call her." My mama called, and I could tell by her face she was blocked as well. Walking to the counter, I grabbed the hospital phone and dialed her number. The nurse tried to stop me, but I gave that hoe a death look that let her know to play with something safe. She didn't answer the phone and panic started to sink in. I had no idea where she lived and her just leaving the hospital let me know she wanted it that way. I know the way a nigga living was whack, but you don't get a nigga back like that. I felt like Jay Z, but I couldn't let the song cry. Them shits fell down my face and I nodded to Lady.

"Let's go." Leaving the hospital, we headed to the airport and I felt defeated. I couldn't believe Raven hated me that much that she would walk away with my child like that. It's like I could still feel the baby in my arms. Not knowing if I was gone ever see her again broke my heart. This bitch Raven had me ready to kill her ass behind this shit. Lady always said it's a thin line.

****

2 MONTHS LATER...

Getting up out of the bed, I looked at the picture Lady printed out of me, Dalia, and Raven. Picking it up, I kissed my daughter and put the picture back down. It's what I did every day since Raven took her away from me. I had been blowing her up until she up and changed the number on my ass. It was nothing else I could do and that's what fucked with me. I went to the warehouse every day, even though I turned everything over to Geno. I just needed to occupy my mind, so I wouldn't do anything stupid. San kept calling me, but I had absolutely nothing to say to

that bitch. She was the reason I was in this shit in the first place.

My doorbell rang, and I was about to beat the breaks off San. I'm

sure it was her, because no one else would just show up to my

shit like that. Running down the stairs, I snatched the door open,

only to find Raven standing there with my daughter. I grabbed my

baby fast as fuck and just squeezed her as tight as I could.

"Hey daddy's baby. Did you miss me? You missed me baby

girl." Looking at her, a nigga eyes watered up because she looked

just like a nigga. Her eyes were open, and she was looking me

dead in the eyes. "That's right, look at your fine ass daddy. That's

who you like." Hugging her again, I couldn't do shit but smile as I

held her. When I finally looked up at Raven, she had this dumb ass

grin on her face that I wanted to wipe off. Moving out the way, I

let her in and walked over to my couch. Unwrapping the baby, I

couldn't help the love that came ripping through me.

"How long you been here?" Raven took her coat off and

sat down across from me.

233

"We just got in." It's like we really didn't know what to say to each other. How do best friends end up here?

"Where you gone be staying at Raven? Would hate for you to up and disappear again." It was a low blow, but that shit was low what she did.

"I'm not sure. My mama's house sold, so I can't stay there. I'm not even sure how long I will be in town. I just wanted you to be able to see her." Grabbing my phone, I threw it to her.

"Put your new number in there." Laughing, she did what I asked, but I didn't find shit funny. "Look, I know I know I fucked up, but I don't deserve this type of hurt. I miss you and I miss my baby. Just stay for a while, with me. Please, let me get to know her and get the chance to wake up with her there. Please, I'll do anything." She just smiled at me.

RAVEN...

I know what I did was fucked up, but I wasn't ready to deal with Rogue. I needed to deal with him on my own terms and when I was ready. Him showing up to the hospital was not on my terms. I gave him the opportunity to watch his child be born and spend two days with her, then I had to go. I needed time to breathe and figure out what I wanted to do. Yes, I love Rogue, but sometimes, love isn't enough. My ass needed time to heal. I'm not all the way there, but I'm at the point where I can try to do the right thing.

Coi and aunt Cheryl was upset because they didn't want Dalia out of their sight. They were like you better call him and make him come here, but I didn't want that. I still didn't want Rogue to know where I lived. I had no idea how long I would be here, but I wanted to give him time with Dalia. Seeing how he stared at her, I knew it was the right decision. His entire being lit up when he saw it was me. I almost felt like shit when I saw how he was.

"We'll stay for a while. Don't get it twisted though, I'm not here to be your girlfriend. I'm only here for your daughter. We will stay in your guest room. I'm considering moving back here or you can move there. Depends on how well this goes while we are here. If that's something that you may want." Rogue jumped up and grabbed me. He poured out so much love in that hug, I was happy that I came.

"I'll do whatever you want me to. Just don't leave with my baby again. Please." Getting up, I went upstairs to use the bathroom. His ass was getting me wet just being around him and I knew I was going to go back on my word. As much as I loved to say I hated him, and I was done, I loved that nigga with all of me. He would always have my heart, but I had to try and protect myself this time.

Even though I told him not to try anything, I really wanted him to. That would let me know that he still wanted me as much as I did him. I had no idea what his situation was, but I've never wanted him more. That's why I had to stay away from him. I didn't trust myself enough to just be around him and not ride his dick. Just in case he came at me, I needed to be ready. My ass knew if his lips hit me, that pussy was gone.

236

Reaching up on his towel rack, I had to do a move from back in the day. Grabbing a towel, I ran some water and put a lil soap on it. Pulling my pants down, I did a quick hoe bath to take away the sweat from the trip here. I didn't want that nigga to go down there and eat gym sock pussy. Not wanting him to know I freshened up, I folded the towel and hid it. Laughing at myself, I walked back out and headed downstairs. I stopped dead in my tracks.

"Rogue, we need to talk about the baby. I know you don't think I will ever allow us to be apart from each other. We have years in this shit." This hoe San was standing there, and I saw Red. I was so sick of this bitch I could punch this hoe in her pussy. "Wow. This bitch again." Laughing, I refused to give in to this hoe. Well, I was trying not to.

"Watch your mouth San. I need for you to get out of my house. Give me my key and leave." Grabbing Dalia's blanket, I shook my head at the fact that this bitch had a key. I was so disappointed in Rogue at this point. I was hurt all over again.

237

"Fuck that bitch. You not gone be satisfied until I drag that hoe." Not about to take shit else off that hoe, I punched the bitch in her mouth so hard, she couldn't do shit but fold. Grabbing my daughter, I wrapped her so fast, she looked like the Taliban.

"Raven wait." Not waiting for him to say another word, I ran the fuck out of there and jumped in my car. Driving off, I left him in the driveway chasing me. This nigga wasn't gone ever change. Did he think I was gone go through this shit forever with this bitch? How the fuck was that hoe still pregnant anyway. Raggedy bitch must be carrying Moses.

I had a good mind to go back and run his ass over. I can't believe I just did a hoe bath for this nigga and he was on the same shit from the past. My phone started ringing and it was Lady. I was about to ignore it, but I was pissed, and I needed to take it out on somebody.

"Why you keep calling me on behalf of your dumb ass son. You should have raised him right and we wouldn't be going through this. Stop calling my phone and go worry about your old ass grandbaby that hoe about to have. Leave me the hell alone."

Hanging up, I blocked her ass and her son. I was not about to do

this shit all over again. The past hurt had surfaced, and I was over

it. Crying, I wiped my tears and headed the fuck back home. My

phone rang again, and I was about to go the fuck off until I saw it

was Coi.

"Sis how did it go? That nigga was happy as hell wasn't he.

I think yall gone get back together now. Y'all are the hood Jay and

Beyoncé. Do I need to get another plan to put into motion?" This

hoe was trying to get me the dick and this nigga had constant

pussy.

"I'm on the way back home. Fuck that nigga. I'm done

trying and I'm sorry, his ass can forget he ever met me." You could

hear her sigh and I knew she didn't agree with my decision.

"Aww Raven. What happened now? It seems like y'all just

can't get this shit right for nothing. Every time I have high hopes

for you two dummies, y'all go and fuck it up. You were supposed

to be there letting him spend time with his baby, but you on your way home. What is with that? Turn around and go back." She was disappointed, but I was too.

"Sis, that bitch San used her key to get in his house after I agreed to live with him for a while. He hasn't changed at all. The bitch is still pregnant, and I guess he think we gone be some sister wives or some shit."

"Wait? Who the fuck she giving birth to Benjamin Button? How the hell is that hoe still pregnant?"

"That's what the fuck I said. I'm not about to do this with them Coi. The hoe disrespectful and I tried to knock her teeth through her wind pipe."

"Y'all need to talk sis. I know you don't believe shit he has to say, but that doesn't matter. All that means is you can't be with him in the way that you want to. Him being a father has nothing to do with that. You can stay with Lady."

"Girl, fuck her too." Coi laughed and I couldn't do shit but laugh with her. I know Lady didn't do shit to me, but I was mad at her bitch ass son. I loved her, all she has ever done was be nice to

240

me. I would love for her to be in Dalia's life, but that would only put me right back around Rogue. This shit was a mess and I was just over it at this point. I couldn't take any more hurt from Rogue.

SAN...

Everyone treated me like I was the bad guy, but they seemed to forget that Rogue pushed me into doing the shit I did. He set off a chain of events and now we all were hurt behind the shit. Knowing Rogue like I do, I know he didn't mean to hurt anyone, but at the end of the day, he did. That nigga embarrassed me in front of everyone I knew. They all treated me like the nasty hoe and didn't want to be bothered with me. Even Jen wouldn't answer or return my calls.

She was the one that had me out here playing this game. I could have aborted the baby in the beginning now that I think about it and not have myself in that position. I think that is what hurt him the most. We may have been able to get past the

241

indiscretions, but the baby killed me out. I've never been so embarrassed in my life. Not having any money or him to pay my rent, I was back living in my mama's house. She barely wanted to fuck with me and no one else would say two words to me. I had no other choice but to come crawling back to Rogue.

Even if he didn't want me, I needed some help. Using my key, I walked in his house. He was holding a baby that looked just like him and my heart stopped. When I looked over and saw that bitch, my blood started boiling. I hated this hoe's entire existence. My mouth went off and the bitch hit me so hard, I had to catch my wig. By the time I had it on straight, she was gone, and Rogue was chasing her. When his ass walked in the door and slammed it, I had to pray.

"WHY THE FUCK ARE YOU HERE? I thought I made myself clear when I told you to stay the fuck away from me. I'm trying not to be that nigga that takes a mother away from her child, but bitch you pushing me to the limit. You about to get put under and it would be smart for you to get away from me."

242

"Rogue, I just needed to talk to you. I know you hate me, and you don't want me, but I need your help. I lost the house, and nobody will fuck with me after the tape you showed them. The baby is on the way here and I just want to know if you will give me a little help. Can I have some of the money we took from Slim?" His ass started laughing hard as hell.

"You want me to give you some money from the nigga you was fucking, and ended up pregnant by? Am I clear on that?"

"I know it's fucked up to ask you that, but please, I really need it."

"I'll bring it by your mom's house later. Get the fuck out of my shit." Even though he said he was, I could look in his face and tell that nigga wasn't about to give me a dime. Defeated, I walked out the door and went to my mama's. As soon as I walked in the door, she was waiting on me and started in.

"You have to get out of here San. I'm not helping you raise no baby. I don't have no money to be giving yall and let's be honest. I don't trust you around my nigga. You crossed the line

243

and I'm sorry, you can't stay here. You have two days to figure out what you gone do."

"Ma, how you gone put me out. You know I don't have anywhere to go. I would never sleep with your man, please don't do this."

"It's already done. Your bags in the garage waiting on you. Like I said, you got two days to get the fuck out of here." She walked off and left me there devastated. I couldn't believe that I was sitting here with nothing. All the years I was with Rogue, my dumb ass wasn't smart enough to save some money. I always thought we would be together, and I wouldn't need to. My mama's boyfriend walked around the corner smiling at me and I didn't find shit funny. He sat on the couch and stared at me.

"I heard you out here a broke hoe. Your mama done put you out and now your lil nasty ass got to get out with your lil bastard baby. What you gone do San?" This nigga was so disrespectful I was ready to beat his ass.

"None of your fucking business. I'll figure it the fuck out on my own. When I get back on, I don't want none of you mufuckas to say a word to me."

"Girl shut up. I can help you. It won't be much, but I can give you something that will last you for a few months. Give you some time to figure out what you gone do. I still got my old apartment and you can take the lil bastard baby there." Even though he was still being disrespectful, I couldn't believe he was willing to help me.

"Oh my God Hank. Thank you so much. I literally had nowhere to go."

"I know and if you really want to thank me, you know what you can do." When he pulled his pants down and started stroking his dick, I wanted to die. What the fuck kind of bitch would I be to fuck my mama's man? His ass knew I was in a desperate situation and used that shit against me. Shaking my head, I wiped the tears from my eyes. Fuck her, she was just about to put me out. A bitch was desperate just like he thought and desperate times, called for

245

desperate measures. Walking over to him, I got on my knees and looked him in the eyes.

"This what you want?" When my mouth hit his dick, he moaned.

"Yes, suck this mufucka." That's just what the fuck I did. I was sucking because my life depended on it. This nigga started moaning so hard, I just knew my mama was going to hear him. "Go in the bathroom, I need some of this pussy." Getting up, I walked to the bathroom and pulled my pants down. As soon as he slid inside of me, he started pumping like crazy. We may as well stayed on the couch because this nigga was screaming and slapping my ass like he was supposed to be in here fucking me. Knowing I needed his help, I threw this ass back and didn't give a fuck if she heard me or not. Her ass didn't give a fuck about me and my baby, so fuck her too. His dick was a nice size and the shit felt good, so fuck it. Hell, if I needed to, I will fuck this nigga every month until I got myself back on track. She better hope I didn't take his ass from her, just to spite her. His ass was grabbing my titties and slamming into me like he was trying to make an exit hole. Hoping that bitch heard me, I allowed all my moans and screams to escape my mouth.

"Yes Hank, fuck this pussy. This is yours daddy, yes baby fuck me. Don't stop, I'm about to cum all on this dick."

"Cum for daddy. I wanna feel you cum." My body started shaking and he pulled out and started sucking my pussy until I came in his mouth. Turning me around, he pushed his dick in my mouth and started pumping like it was my pussy. It felt like my mouth was splitting, but I took that shit.

"Ahhhh fuck." Snatching his dick out of my mouth, he sprayed his nut all over my face. Licking around my mouth, I stared him in his eyes as I placed kisses on his dick.

"Next time, come by the apartment and I can fuck you right. I promise you will never want another pussy fucking with me." His ass started laughing and put his dick in his pants.

"How the fuck am I gone pay for another apartment? Your mama take care of me. I ain't got no fucking money or another place. Shit sounded good though didn't it? Your mama was right, you are a nasty bitch that would fuck her man. Shit was good as fuck too. Maybe I could convince her to let you stay here so I can get that pussy anytime I want. Hell if I beat her ass good enough or threaten to leave, maybe I can fuck both of yall at the same time. If nothing else, I got two more days. Keep that pussy clean for me, I'll be back tonight." For the first time in my life, I was speechless. This bitch ass nigga played me, and I did exactly what everyone thought I would. That's why nobody would fuck with me and I had no one to turn to. Pulling my clothes up, I got up and went in the kitchen. Grabbing a knife, I walked in my room. Locking the door, I sat on the bed and sliced my wrists. Jamming the knife in my throat, I cried as I bled out. It was no coming back from the low I had just hit.

FOREVER DON'T LAST

ROGUE…

After San left, I went to my safe and counted out two

hundred thousand dollars. No she wasn't carrying my baby, but I

had the money of the nigga's it was. It was only right I gave her

enough for her shorty to be straight. All of this shit was my fault

and I could accept that. I had a weakness for kids and that baby

didn't deserve to suffer because the mama wasn't shit. After I

packed it up, I stopped by Lady's house to let her know what was

going on. When I got in the door, she was looking worse than me.

Us losing Dalia had us fucked up. Even though she still dealt with

me because I was her child, I could tell she blamed me. It just

wasn't the same between us.

"Lady, I saw Dalia." Her face lit up and you would think it

was her child.

"Oh my God, where did you see her? Why the fuck you

didn't bring her over here or take me with you?"

"Raven showed up at my door with the baby. I convinced her to live with me for a while and let us get to know the baby. She said yeah."

"Again nigga, why the fuck you didn't bring her over here?"

"If you shut your bald headed ass up, I will tell you. San showed up saying she needed to talk about the baby. Raven grabbed Dalia and ran out of the door. She won't answer, and I don't know where she went." Grabbing her phone, she called Raven. All she got out was hello and then she was laying the phone down.

"That bitch disrespectful." When she laughed, I knew Lady had a soft spot for her. She didn't let nobody talk to her the way Raven had been talking to her. "You better find her and make it right."

"I am mama. Let me make this run real quick and I'm going to try and find Raven, so I can explain to her what the fuck is going on." Getting up, I jumped in my car and headed to San's mama

250

house. When I got there, it was police cars everywhere. Jumping out, I walked inside, and her mama was sitting there looking shocked.

"Ma, what happened?"

"She killed herself. They took her because they are trying to save the baby." I was confused on why she was still here.

"Come ride with me. What hospital did they take her to?"

"County." Getting up, she came with me like she really didn't want to. When we got in the car, I needed to know what the hell happened.

"Why you acting like you don't care? Why did she kill herself?" My emotions were all over the place. Even though San was foul, I was with her for years and I couldn't believe she was gone.

"Rogue, do you know how it feels to sit there and listen to your daughter fuck your man in your house and she knew you were there? Well, I do and that's what I just went through. The only reason she killed herself is because she found out Hank was lying. He couldn't give her money or help her. Knowing she had no one else to turn to, she killed herself. I went in there to put her out and she was bleeding everywhere."

"Where the fuck is Hank?"

"In the house. What was he supposed to do, and she threw the sex at him? Men will be men." This mufucka had lost her mind. I'm glad I had the mama that I did, because bitches like her needed to be six feet. When we got to the hospital, we waited for the doctor to come out. When he finally did, he told us he was able to save the baby. They wanted to know who would be raising it, and I told them we would let them know. I still couldn't believe San was gone.

"I have two hundred thousand dollars I was about to give to San. If you take the baby, the money is yours, but that nigga Hank gotta go. I don't trust him around the baby and you shouldn't either. You stay here and wait on the baby. I'm going to go back to your house to see if the police are gone. If they are, I will make Hank leave and the money will be there.

Getting up, I walked out and had to fight back tears. This shit was beginning to be too much, and it all started from a mistake I made. Had I just been honest with everyone, maybe I could have avoided all this shit. My mind was heavy when I got back to San's mama house. The police were gone, and I was happy about that. I never wanted to deal with them on any level. Walking through the house, I looked for Hank. When I found him sleeping, I woke his ass up with a hit over his head. That nigga jumped up looking stupid.

"What the fuck are you doing?" Grabbing him, I pointed the gun at his head.

"We're going for a ride. Don't worry about your stuff, you won't be going anywhere. You have about thirty more minutes left on this earth. Say your prayers Hank. Say your prayers." His ass damn near shitted on his self when, but I didn't give a fuck. I knew if I left him alive, San's mom would go back to him. I couldn't allow that nigga around the baby. What he did was borderline rape and I couldn't have that. Driving him to the

253

warehouse, I made him get out and walked him inside. Geno was looking at me like I was crazy.

"My nigga just can't stay away from the life. You sure you don't want back in? We can be partners in this shit. It's enough bread for us both." That's why I fucked with that nigga. He wasn't greedy.

"Naw, but I need you to do something else for me. This nigga here like taking pussy and lying to get it. I need him to disappear." Geno laughed.

"I got booty thief. Gone and get out of here. You know there will be no evidence left behind." I knew Geno was like me because I trained him.

"Good looking. I'll holla at you later. I see you out here getting it and shit boss man, we'll link up." That nigga shrugged like he was still struggling.

"I'm just trying to make it out here. You the one that got it." Shaking my head, I laughed and walked out.

254

"Nigga you just trying to get out of buying drinks. Cheap ass. When we link, everything on you my nigga."

"Aight nigga you got it. You fed me for years. Least I can do is get you a five dollar box." Laughing, I walked out on his ass. Getting in my car, I headed back to Lady's house. I needed to tell her what happened to San. I knew she was gone say the shit was on me, and in a way it was. Granted, San didn't have to turn out the way she did. She made the decision to cross and burn bridges. I can admit I set the shit in motion, but the way she went about it was wrong. I prayed that baby came out on top, but it was no way I was raising it.

Right now, I couldn't dwell on the shit I could have done differently. All I can do is change how I was from this moment on. I needed to find Raven and make this shit right. Tonight just showed me how shit can happen that fast. I was gone make it right, I just needed her to wait for me.

WAIT

RAVEN...

It's been three months since I last walked out on Rogue.
Dalia was getting big and she looked so much like him, it was
scary. It was a constant reminder of him and no matter how hard I
tried to forget, I was reminded of him every day. They hadn't
called my phone anymore and I didn't have to change my number
this time around. I was starting to feel badly about taking the
baby. My feelings shouldn't have affected him seeing his child, but
I was hurt. I needed some time to myself and I got it. My mind
was made up and I was going to call him tomorrow.

Going to my closet, I looked through my clothes and found
the perfect dinner dress. I was about to go to dinner and I needed
the perfect look. Grabbing my white fitted button up and black
pencil skirt, I put it on and made sure I looked perfect. Sliding on
my black So Kate red bottom heels, I grabbed my red Louboutin
purse and I was ready to go. Coi was on her way over here to

watch Dalia, so that I could go out. She was such a true blessing, but it was time for her to stop being the baby daddy and just be the God mother.

"Where my chunky chocolate baby? Come here baby D, come to your real mama." I laughed as Coi went straight for the baby as soon as she came in. Bitch didn't even say hi to me or nothing.

"Well hello to you too. You're early, you must have been bored as hell."

"Naw, I needed to talk to you. Before you get mad, I just need you to hear me out."

"Here we go. I'm listening."

"I think you should talk to Rogue." I tried to stop her and let her know I planned on it.

"Coi..."

"Don't cut me off. Let me finish and then you can talk. You and that man have been through hell and back since yall were kids. When you had nobody else, you had him. Did you know he used to give you his money and then had to go steal to feed his

self? That nigga went without every day, just so you could have.

I'm sure you also didn't know, the day he got locked up, is

because he was trying to rob a gas station to give you money. He's

always had your back. When you were raped, nobody believed

you but me and my mom.

Those bastards got away scott free. The minute you told

him, they ass was no longer with us. Now I know yall may never

work as a couple, but don't walk away from a friendship like

yours. If nothing else, my beautiful baby was created from that.

Call him and hear him out. He deserves that much." By the time

she finished, my ass was crying. I didn't know any of that and that

made him even more special to me. My phone rung and I saw it

was a Chicago number. I knew it had to be him.

"It's Rogue." She mouthed answer it and I did. "Hello."

"Raven, I need to see you and my baby. Can I please come

and talk to you face to face? I promise it's not what you think. Just

let me come see you." My pussy started thumping.

"You can come. Where are you now?" I would give him my address once he made it to Atlanta.

"I'm right here." The goosebumps on my arms stood up and I knew he was in my room. Turning around, I was face to face with Rogue. It's a damn shame how my pussy betrays me every time he came around.

"Good, you can babysit Dalia while I go to dinner. You two need to bond. It's nice to see you Rogue, but if you fall asleep, take your ass in the guest room."

"You really gone leave without hearing me out? Raven we need to fix this Shorty. You going out with another nigga is not the answer." On the inside I was cracking up. He was jealous. This was a business meeting with my publisher. Not a personal date.

"We'll talk tomorrow, don't wait up. Where is Lady, I'm surprised she's not here. She could have kept you company."

"I'm right here. I stayed outside just in case your ass got disrespectful. I didn't want to beat your ass." Laughing, I hugged her and kissed her cheek. I was sorry for the way I had been treating her.

"I'm sorry Lady. Blame your big head son. Now, I have to leave. Coi, you know where I am if there are any problems." Leaving out, I jumped in my car and pulled off. Even though Coi ass had been talking to them behind my back, I was glad she did. It was time for us to bury the hatchet. Pulling up to Ruth's Chris, I gave my keys to valet and walked inside. I couldn't wait to get some of this steak.

Me and my publisher was eating and discussing my new ventures I was working on when my phone rung. Coi was calling and I panicked. Letting him know I had to take the call, I picked up.

"Is everything okay? What's wrong with the baby sis? I'm on the way now. Just tell me she is okay."

"Sis she is fine." Taking a deep breath, I relaxed. "Umm you may be upset with me, but I kind of told Rogue where you were at and he is on his way there."

"WHAT!!!" Everyone turned and looked at me and I tried to quiet down. "Why would you do that? I'll see you when I get home." Hanging up, I turned to my publisher to tell his ass we needed to get out of there when the goosebumps arrived. It was too late.

"From the moment that I knew what love was, I loved you. I have messed up more times than I can count, trying to get it right. I'm sorry for all the hurt that I caused you, but I need you to stand still. Let me prove to you that I can be the man you need. Shorty, I need you to wait for me. All I wanna do is work it out with you. Give a nigga a chance to make it up to you." If I was on a real date, I would have left that nigga quick. With tears in my eyes, I nodded my head yes. Running towards him, I leaped in his arms and kissed him with all of my heart on the line.

Everyone in the room started clapping and I couldn't believe he did that in front of all those people. Using his fingers, he wiped the tears from my face and kissed me again. I knew we had a long road ahead of us, but my heart belonged to him. It was

261

no doubt about that. Even though it was petty for me to leave, it made him see the error in the shit he did. Turning to my publisher we both laughed.

"Rogue this is my publisher. I was at a business meeting. It's good to know you were jealous and thought I was moving on though." Dropping his head, he began to laugh. Walking over they shook hands and he sat down with us. Even though I had to finish my meeting, I was barely listening. I couldn't stop wondering if Rogue was going to fuck me once we got back home. My pussy was throbbing, and I needed this meeting to be over. My publisher finally caught the hint and told us to get out of there. When valet brought my Audi sports car to me, I took off like a bat out of hell. He had a ways to go to make this shit up, but right now my pussy needed some healing. My heart could wait.

ROGUE...

When I dropped off the bitch ass nigga Hank to Geno, I went back to Lady's house. She was devastated when I told her what happened. The look in her face was kind of a mix between disappointment and blame. She silently told me I fucked up

everyone's life. She didn't have to say it, her eyes did.

"Lady I know what you're thinking. I know I fucked up, but

the shit wasn't on purpose. I really thought I was doing the right

thing. I have no control over what happened to San. That is done."

"Son I know you didn't mean it. There is a lesson in all of

this. I'm hoping it does not end with us not ever seeing Dalia, but

we have to take whatever is to come." You could see the tears

about to fall and I knew I had to fix it.

"Ma, what you think about moving to Atlanta?" She

jumped up and ran upstairs. I had no idea what she was doing

until she came downstairs carrying her purse and her wig.

"I don't need none of this shit. Just my good hair and ID.

You ready?"

"Yeah, when we get there, I have a plan. We won't see

Dalia for a few months, but I'm going to fix it. Just trust me. I'll be

back and forth to make sure everything is handled here. I have to

get my money to Atlanta as well, but for now, we out of here."

263

"Bitch if you get me out here on a whim and don't know what you doing, imma beat your ass. You better have a plan and shit." Laughing, we got in my car and drove to the airport.

As soon as we landed, I called Coi and explained everything to her. By the time I finished the complete story, I knew I had her on my side. After telling her my plan, she was in tears. I couldn't come to Raven half stepping anymore. When she saw me, I would have everything in order.

Three months later, I was ready. I called Coi and she gave me the address. I was taking a chance, but I prayed she would hear me out. When shorty said yes, I walked in. What I didn't expect was for her to be taking her funky ass on a date. That shit had me feeling fucked up, but I was in no position to argue with her. The last thing I needed was for her to run with Dalia again. I was in Raven's court, but I knew how to play ball. Coi tried to act as if she was playing with the baby, but I wasn't having it.

"Do you want to be the person that stands in the way of true love? You know me, and Shorty belong together. All I need is a shot with no interference this time. If she finishes this date, that puts us in another fucked up predicament. Someone else will be hurt, and the cycle continues."

"I agree with you nigga. You preaching to the choir. Especially after I felt what you were working with, I want you all up in my sister's life." Lady turned around looking at us confused. We both laughed, and she knew it had to be harmless. "She will be pissed if I tell you where she is. I'm surprised I didn't get it for giving out this mufucka.

"Coi, if you know we supposed to be together, what's the point of the date? No more hurting innocent people. Tell me where she is, and I'll make it up to you." You could see her thinking it over.

"I'll tell you on one condition. You have to step into the hallway though. Mama Lady don't need to see this." I laughed because I knew she was on some bullshit. Walking in the hallway, I waited for her demand. "Whip that bad boy out and let me see what it looks like out of clothes." Shaking my head, I knew it was gone be some freaky shit. Her ass was bat shit crazy and Raven found this shit funny as hell.

"You want me to do what? Coi, you done already grabbed it, rubbed it, and stroked the mufucka. What more do you want? I'm sure. You know exactly what's down there." She fell the fuck out, so I thought I was in the clear.

"I know I felt it, that's why I want to see it. If you want this address, you will whip it out. The longer you take, the closer she is to going home giving him that pussy." Coi ass wasn't shit. She was laughing hard as hell at my expense. Shaking my head, I grabbed my dick and pulled it out. Of my jogging pants.

"You good now?"

"Damn mufucka. That bitch just flopped down like it was too heavy. Sheit." Reaching over, this crazy mufucka grabbed my shit again and shook her head. "Plus, the shit is soft. Put that shit up. You walking around with a deadly weapon. I'll text you the address. I'm going home to fuck the shit out of my husband after seeing this shit. Nigga got an urban myth in his pants." This girl

266

was mumbling as she walked off about my dick. I swear I don't

know how Raven put up with her. If I didn't know that's how she

was, I would have thought the bitch was flaw and trying to fuck.

"Lady, keep Dalia. Coi is gone and I'm going to get Raven.

You're here by yourself with her."

"I got her." Running down the stairs, I jumped in my truck

and headed downtown. Next thing I know, I'm standing there

pouring my heart out for her to choose me and the nigga was her

boss. Me knowing my shorty, the way she moved out of there let

me know she wanted the dick. My ass was back in my truck racing

her to the house. When she went in the garage, I parked in the

front and ran inside.

Looking all over the house, I couldn't find her. I knew she

was there, because I saw her go inside. What the fuck. Walking to

the garage door, I went inside. She was lying on top of her Audi in

just her panties, bra and heels. My dick stood up and I freed him

instantly. I never thought I would see the day I was going back in

this pussy. Grabbing her legs, I pushed them back all the way to her face. Licking her clit through her panties, I teased the shit out of her. Sucking gently on her clit through her panties, she screamed out in agony. Moving them to the side, I started sucking the shit out of that pussy. Sliding my finger in and out of her while I sucked on that clit, my dick damn near bust feeling her juices coat my fingers. I needed to feel it.

Climbing on top of the car, I slid my dick inside of her. I should have known from the first time I fucked her that I wouldn't want to fuck nobody else. We were the perfect fit and our bodies was in sync. When she first left, my ass used to dream about her. With each stroke, I tried to make her feel my love and how sorry I was. I would never hurt her again and I needed her to feel that shit in her soul. Her body started shaking and she came all over my shit.

Since she got her nut from me making love to her, I balled her ass up and slid her down the car. Now it was time to beat that shit up. I had her arms and legs on lock and she couldn't do shit but take the dick. Each time my dick went deeper, that mufucka got harder. It felt like my shit was about to explode and then it did. I had never cum that hard before in my life. Releasing her arms and legs, I leaned down and kissed her.

"I love you Shorty."

"I love you too Rogue. Now tell me, how the fuck did you get Coi to tell you where I was?" Laughing, I dropped my head in shame.

"I had to show her my dick. She grabbed that mufucka then went home to fuck her man. She sold your ass out quick once she saw it." Raven fell out laughing and I loved that sound more than anything.

"I knew it. That girl asked me damn near every day to see a pic of your dick. She is something else. Come on, let's go in the house and check on our baby girl. That shit was music to my ears and I couldn't wait. Walking in the house, Lady was in the kitchen getting some water.

"Yall a bunch of nasty mufuckas. I'm definitely gone need my own shit. I refuse to listen to Raven screaming like that every

269

time yall doing it. Damn shame. Take a shower before you go

picking my grand baby up." Laughing, we walked past her to go

upstairs.

"Yes ma'am." As soon as I hit the first step, Raven jumped

on my back.

"I'm high, you know I can't walk when I'm high." Shaking

my head at her faking ass, I carried her up the stairs.

WE BELONG TOGETHER

RAVEN...

I know I said that we had some things to work out, but everything was perfect. I never thought Rogue and I would be back here, but I was so happy that he didn't give up on us, even when I did. He was everything and I couldn't be more in love. My ass just walked around singing and smiling for no damn reason. Standing over them, I looked at how beautiful my family was. Dalia was lying on top of Rogue and they were knocked out sleep. Grabbing my phone, I started snapping pictures to post on Facebook.

"That's some creep shit. How you gone be just taking all them pics and he don't know it?" When I looked at Coi, I fell the fuck out. She was talking shit but staring at his print. "How the hell is that mufucka that big and it's lying there sleep? I think I hear that bitch snoring. That shit is just beautiful." Cracking up laughing, I shook my head at her.

"I'm glad he sleeps in draws with your nasty ass."

"I'm glad they're briefs with my nasty ass. Shit is picture perfect. Anyway, what you got planned for today?"

"Me and Rogue supposed to go look at a house, WHEN HE WAKES HIS ASS UP." I made sure I screamed the last part in attempt to wake his ass up. He didn't move. Coi went and grabbed Dalia off his chest.

"You know how to wake that ass up. Get to work."

"Girl. We ain't did shit in days. These walls too thin. Lady can hear us when we fuck. So the only time we get it in, is when we get a quickie in the car somewhere else. She even heard us in the garage. My pussy dying." Her ass laughed, but it wasn't funny.

"Sis, getting another house ain't gone change that. I'll die if I couldn't fuck my husband. Yall crazy. Lady ass would be on the porch."

"Lady ass will be beating they ass if they tried." We fell out when Lady responded through the walls. I told her these mufuckas was thin. I never noticed that, because I was always here by myself.

"I'm going to let her have this house and me and Rogue is going to find a new one. You know start from scratch together."

"Awwww I'm so happy for you sister. Well, I'm about to take Dalia with me. I'll see yall later. Get him up, so yall can go find a house. That shit creepy fucking with your mama in law listening." I laughed as she walked out with the baby. I never had to pack her a bag because she had everything at her house as well. This lil girl was spoiled as hell, everyone wanted her all the time.

Knowing I had to be quiet, I climbed in the bed and slipped his dick out of his briefs. I knew I couldn't go hard because I needed his ass to stay quiet. Kissing the tip of his dick, I laughed when it jumped. Slowly taking the tip in my mouth, I went down slowly. Making sure my mouth was wet as hell, I gave him the wet vac. All suction with sloppy ass spit. I knew he was woke, because I kept feeling his toes curl. He didn't make a sound, but when his vein started bulging, it was hard for him to contain it. Rogue bit the fuck out of his lip as his body rose up off the bed. Once he came, I kept sucking and he pushed my head back.

"Your ass don't play fair. I'm up." Licking my lips, I smiled at him as we walked in the bathroom to handle our hygiene. Turning the shower water on, we took our clothes off and I got ready to climb inside. His ass pushed me down and I held onto the tub as he entered me slowly. It was a damn shame our ass was out here sneaking like some teenagers.

Knowing we couldn't be loud, he slow stroked me. That shit made it harder to be quiet. If the water wasn't on, all you would have heard was my pussy talking. That shit was wet as hell and I could tell it was hard for him not to beat it up. That nigga had a death grip on my ass but was moving slowly. I started twisting my hips and throwing it back. Our pace increased, but he still managed to not make that slapping noise. My body started shaking and I came, five minutes later, he was cumming inside of me.

274

"We gotta find a house today. I'm a grown ass man sneaking pussy." We climbed in and washed each other up. Thirty minutes later, we were getting dressed. We had our areas narrowed down, but we weren't in agreeance. His ass wanted to live in Buckhead, but it was very expensive over there. I let him convince me to go look, but I had my mind made up. We got downstairs and Lady was dressed like she was going somewhere as well.

"Lady, you look like you about to hit the town as well. What you got going on?"

"I'm going with you mufuckas. I don't know this place or these people. Yall done made me move out here, so yall gotta deal with my ass going where yall go. Hey best friend go best friend." I laughed, but I was low key pissed. I wanted to get some dick in the car. Her ass was blocking in the house and now on our road trips. Rogue didn't suck this pussy and I needed it shit.

"Well alright. I guess we all looking at houses today. Just know yall not about to gang up on me and shit." Lady put her hand to her neck as if she was clutching her pearls.

"It's other way around. Men don't have no taste. We gone have to talk him into some shit together. We need to get this show on the road hell. I'm in a new city, I'm trying to find me a man too." We high fived and Rogue didn't like that.

"Well if you looking for a man, your bald head ass better go upstairs and get your hair. You done forgot it on the dresser." When her hand went up to her head in shock, I fell the fuck out.

"Good looking son. They would have thought I was trying to sell them socks and towels. Hold on, I'll be right back. Don't leave me." As soon as she went upstairs, I whispered to Rogue.

"Come on, let's leave her ass. I'm trying to get this cat ate like Ming Ling's Chow Low Mein." His ass laughed and shook his head no.

"I don't eat Chinese. WE ARE NOT LEAVING LADY LIL NASTY." His ass screamed the last part to get me in trouble. When

276

she came back downstairs putting her hair on, she flung it and hit

me in the face with it.

"You ain't shit." Lady was playing mad.

"I'm sorry mama, but his ass owes me. Come on, let's just

go find this damn house." Leaving out, we got in his truck and

headed to find our dream house.

ROGUE...

As we headed to go look at this house, I thought about all

that we had been through and overcome. It was crazy how I

thought I would never see her again just months ago. The first

night here after we made love, I told her everything. San's

cheating, me killing the nigga and leaving the game, San faking

being pregnant by me, and her killing herself. She was horrified

and couldn't believe I had been going through all of that.

Of course she felt bad that she wasn't there for me and

was mad at me for nothing. I told her none of that shit mattered

because we found our way back to each other. All that mattered was the now. I'm not gone lie though, it broke me when I found out she was about to kill my baby. I would forever be grateful to Coi for having her back the way that she did.

Everything was perfect except our living arrangement. Lady ass had to go, because I needed to tear that pussy up. It wasn't long before we were in the Kingswood neighborhood. Raven was looking out the window and I couldn't do shit but smile.

"Oh my God. That lady back there was holding a big ass sign that said Raven." She kept looking back and I stopped the car to try and see what she was talking about.

"I don't see nothing. I'm sure ain't nobody asking for change out here. You tweaking."

"I'm not crazy. They weren't asking for change, it said Raven."

"Aww ok." She shook her head when she realized I didn't believe her.

"Will. Who the fuck is Will. That man holding a sign that says will. Why are they out here with cards that has people names on it? We in that Get out neighborhood. They gone try to kill me, we can't stay here. Fuck that." I looked back but saw nothing.

"Baby are you okay? What the hell are you talking about?" She kept looking back, but I kept driving.

"You? Who the hell would name their child You? You can turn this car around. That's what YOU can do. I'm not living over here. These mufuckas weird." The next sign was coming up and I got ready. "Marry? OH MY GOD. RAVEN WILL YOU MARRY..." And right there was the last sign that said me. It was in front of a big dumb ass five bedroom house. She turned around to look at me and I had the ring in my hand. Getting out of the car, I walked around and opened her door.

"Raven you're my best friend and I can't imagine my life without you in it. Since we could walk, you have been right there by my side. I'm a movement by myself, but I'm a force when we're together. You complete me and now, I'm ready to make your world complete. Will you marry me?" When I got down on my knees, she got down with me.

"Yes baby, I will." Coi big mouth ass started screaming as soon as we kissed. Raven looked around and was shocked to see her and Dalia on the lawn.

"That day I came to your house, I hadn't just got here. Me and Lady was here for three months having our dream house built. Go inside future Mrs. Wright. It's all yours." Shorty didn't even think twice. She took off running and she dragged Coi with her. I had finally gotten my family and a nigga didn't want anything else. A nigga finally had it all.

THE END...

EACH CHAPTER WAS NAMED AFTER A SONG. TURN THE PAGE FOR A COPY OF THE PLAYLIST.

OH AND BE ON THE LOOKOUT FOR MY NEXT SERIES.

BLAZE MEETS PHANTOM IN THE "SON OF A CRIME GOD." YOU ARE NOT READY FOR THAT TYPE OF CRAZY.

RIGHT AND A WRONG WAY PLAYLIST

MY FIRST LOVE- AVANT

GOD'S PLAN- DRAKE

HEART TO HEART- CHRIS BROWN

IN MY MIND- HEATHER HEADLY

SORRY NOT SORRY- BRYSON TILLER

AS WE LAY- SHIRLEY MURDOCK

BE CAREFUL- CARDI B

INSECURE- JAZMINE SULLIVAN & BRYSON TILLER

SURVIVAL- DRAKE

BABY MAMA DRAMA- DAVE HOLLISTER

NEXT LIFETIME- ERYKA BADU

NO SHAME- FUTURE & PARTY NEXT DOOR

I HATE U, I LOVE U- GNASH

GOSSIP- LIL WAYNE

MONA LISA- LIL WAYNE

YOUR CHILD- MARY J. BLIGE

FOREVER DON'T LAST- JAZMINE SULLIVAN

WAIT- MAROON 5

WE BELONG TOGETHER- MARIAH CAREY

KEEP UP WITH LATOYA NICOLE

Like my author page on fb @misslatoyanicole

My fb page Latoya Nicole Williams

IG Latoyanicole35

Twitter Latoyanicole35

Snap Chat iamTOYS

Reading group: Toy's House of Books

Email latoyanicole@yahoo.com

⍰

OTHER BOOKS BY LATOYA NICOLE

NO WAY OUT: MEMOIRS OF A HUSTLA'S GIRL

NO WAY OUT 2: RETURN OF A SAVAGE

GANGSTA'S PARADISE

GANGSTA'S PARADISE 2: HOW DEEP IS YOUR LOVE

ADDICTED TO HIS PAIN (STANDALONE)

LOVE AND WAR: A HOOVER GANG AFFAIR

LOVE AND WAR 2: A HOOVER GANG AFFAIR

LOVE AND WAR 3: A HOOVER GANG AFFAIR

LOVE AND WAR 4: A GANGSTA'S LAST RIDE

CREEPING WITH THE ENEMY: A SAVAGE STOLE MY HEART PART 1

CREEPING WITH THE ENEMY A SAVAGE STOLE MY HEART PART 2

I GOTTA BE THE ONE YOU LOVE (STANDALONE)

284

THE RISE AND FALL OF A CRIME GOD: PHANTOM AND ZARIA'S STORY

THE RISE AND FALL OF A CRIME GOD 2: PHANTOM AND ZARIA'S STORY

ON THE 12TH DAY OF CHRISTMAS MY SAVAGE GAVE TO ME

A CRAZY KIND OF LOVE: PHANTOM AND ZARIA

14 REASONS TO LOVE YOU: A LATOYA NICOLE ANTHOLOGY

SHADOW OF A GANGSTA

THAT GUTTA LOVE 1

THAT GUTTA LOVE 2

LOCKED DOWN BY HOOD LOVE 1

LOCKED DOWN BY HOOD LOVE 2

THE BEARD GANG CHRONICLES 2 (THE TEASE)

THROUGH THE FIRE: A STANDALONE NOVEL

DAUGHTER OF A HOOD LEGEND

DAUGHTER OF A HOOD LEGEND 2

285

A RUTHLESS KIND OF LOVE

A RUTHLESS KIND OF LOVE 2

A RUTHLESS KIND OF LOVE 3

TAKEN BY A HOOD MENACE: A STANDALONE NOVEL

TIS THE SEASON TO MEND A HITTA'S HEART

AIN'T NO HITTA LIKE THE ONE I GOT 1

AIN'T NO HITTA LIKE THE ONE I GOT 2

⍰

BOOK 34, AND I CAN'T BELIEVE IT. TEN NUMBER ONES, I'M STILL IN DISBELIEF. YOU GUYS ARE AWESOME, AND I LOVE YOU. THANK YOU FOR CONTINOUSLY MAKING MY BOOKS A SUCCESS. WITHOUT YOU THERE IS NO ME. MAKE SURE YOU DOWNLOAD, SHARE, READ AND REVIEW. MORE BOOKS WILL BE COMING FROM ME. BE ON THE LOOK OUT. NO MATTER WHAT HAPPENS, I HOPE YOU ALL WILL CONTINUE TO SUPPORT ME THE SAME. NO MATTER WHAT, I'M STILL LATOYA NICOLE. IT CAN ONLY GET BETTER. TELL A FRIEND TO TELL A FRIEND TO DOWNLOAD MY BOOKS.

CPSIA information can be obtained
at www.ICGtesting.com
Printed in the USA
LVHW111753130819
627498LV00002B/303/P